THE
BROKEN
PLACES

MARIAH K WILLIAMS

Self-published by Mariah K Williams
http://onethreadthatwinds.com/books
onethreadthatwinds@gmail.com

It'll All Work Out
Words and Music by Tom Petty
Copyright (c) 1987 Gone Gator Music
All Rights Reserved Used by Permission
Reprinted by Permission of Hal Leonard Corporation

Cover photography by Gabriel Lungu of G & G Arts
info@gabrielphoto.net

Cover design by Lynn Roach of CaraBella Creative

ISBN: 978-0-9915774-1-5

To my constant encouragers…
without you this would still be
a one-page handwritten "start."

Our parents never told us who was born first. They said our lives began in unison, our hearts beating their first beats in synchronicity. They told us that, as babies, we'd lay in exactly the same position. Our father would set a hand on each of our chests to feel our heartbeats and one would not deviate from the other's pattern. As we grew up, we promised each other never to reveal the time listed on our birth certificates; we didn't want to know who was in the world first. It made us sad to think that one had ever been in the world without the other even if it had been for only moments.

Perhaps this fact is what made the moment so much more painful. I held Daniel's birth certificate for the first time and knew that I'd been the one in the world alone before him... and I was the one alone, again, after him.

ONE

MUD AND MELTED snow, carried from the icy streets in the flood current of snow-delayed commuters and last-minute Christmas shoppers, left the floor of the train station puddled and slick. Sarah couldn't shake the ache in her stomach that had been throbbing and growing since she stepped out of her office that evening.

Ulcers, she told herself. *That's what all this stress and caffeine gets you.*

Sarah tried to call Daniel for the fifth time, angling her phone for optimal signal more out of habit than actual necessity. She reached his voicemail again and, this time, blamed being underground, disregarding the reality that if there was no signal she still wouldn't have reached his voicemail. The train pulled into the station and the crowd swept her towards the opening doors. She resolved to call again when she got up to the street.

The air inside the train felt like summer with the stagnant humid heat of too many bodies crammed into too small a space. She absentmindedly hit redial and heard his voicemail begin for what felt like the millionth time. Two, three, four times she redialed before her stop was announced. Five, six, seven times before the frigid wall of wind and snow took her breath away as she reached the exit of the Columbus Circle station with the throng pouring out onto the street.

Do. Not. Panic. Sarah thought, even as the dull ache in the pit of her stomach spread into a burning knot in her chest. *Don't be stupid. Everything is fine. Nothing to worry about. He's just working and forgot his phone upstairs.* She reached out to him, tugged on the tendrils always connecting their thoughts, but all was quiet. *Or he's asleep. Or high.* Her own mind betrayed her attempt to think the best. The "quiet" was more and more common these days and she was running out of excuses for him.

For as long as Sarah could remember, she and Daniel had an uncanny ability to sense each other. It was more than simple intuition. To her it felt like a secret tunnel linked their two minds with a door at both ends. Most of the time, the doors were left wide open and feelings, thoughts, even visions passed freely and constantly between them. When a door was closed, an echoing emptiness replaced the flow, but like any real door, if she got close enough she could usually sense life within. It took a lot of effort to shut the other out completely; a skill only Daniel had mastered.

Sarah found herself at her apartment door without remembering the walk to her building, the ride up the elevator, or how long she'd been standing there. The calm that usually enveloped her as she left behind the commotion of the city hadn't arrived.

Eleven hours 'til the morning train, she calculated, glancing at her watch. *He's fine. He's fine,* she recited to the reflection of herself in the mirror as she tied her long straight brown hair into a tidy bun. She stared for a moment, isolating her features that match Daniel the most. Their blue eyes framed by thick dark eyebrows, sharp cheekbones with matching angular jaw, nose as straight as an arrow. Sarah smiled to make Daniel's mouth smile back at her then went about packing her things for the long Christmas holiday.

THE TRAIN MOVED slower than usual as it crept along the tracks through the new snow. The trees and buildings were all familiar; she could close her eyes and play the scenery back from memory. Sarah had taken the early train more times than she could remember, but the brown leaves on the branches from her last trip were now replaced by an icing of snow. She gazed, half awake, out the window and thought about the children waking all over the various towns she was passing, elated to find the new blanket of white coating the ground.

The announcement of "White Plains" through the intercom prompted Sarah to pull her heavy winter coat tighter. She flipped up the collar for good measure. Earlier that morning she had frantically raced through Grand Central Station, bags trailing violently behind her tall lean figure, almost missing her train. Slipping into the first car she reached as the doors were closing meant that she now, upon arrival, had the inconvenient fortune of exiting the train at the farthest point of platform from the station. Slowed by the now battered bags of wrapped gifts and her lone rolling suitcase, she stepped out onto the platform and held her breath momentarily as a frigid gust crashed into her, finding every weakness in her clothing and touching skin.

She wished she'd asked him to meet her at the platform. The few people who got off the train before her took any cab that had been waiting and the truck she expected to see parked at the curb wasn't there. Daniel wasn't there.

She stood there for a few minutes, glancing at her phone, first to see if the train arrived early, then again every 10 seconds as if that would somehow make him arrive sooner. No missed calls. Full bars. She tried Daniel's number again, but his voicemail was now full. She thought of all her messages. Frustration began to warm her cheeks as she realized another cab wouldn't come by until the next train arrived and she'd be frozen solid before then. Out of alternatives, she threaded the shopping bags over the handle of her suitcase and set off down the road. The new snow kept the wheels from turning and the dragging case plowed the sidewalk clear behind her.

The nauseating pain in her chest wasn't from paranoid panic, but from irritation. *How could he forget me? If he's been carving at that damn statue, blasting his brain out with his freaking music I'll kill him!* The fury fueled her, adding warmth and adrenaline and she kept a quick pace despite her heavy load.

The walk was just a little over a mile, nothing that would kill her, but annoying nevertheless. She tried to enjoy the airy open feel after the last few weeks spent doing a sardine impression on the streets of New York City. Traffic was sparse since it was still early on Christmas Eve and she distracted herself with the old two-story homes and interspersed storefronts decorated with wreaths and lights.

Daniel's truck was parked at the curb in front of the old hardware store. The snow was inches thick on the windshield and roof yet she could see bare pavement underneath. Immediately, her mental timeline snapped to the previous morning when she noticed the first snowflakes while walking the last block to her office. The truck hadn't moved since before the snow came. Daniel hadn't gone anywhere.

He has friends who have cars, Sarah. Stop reading into things, she rationalized, but her underlying panic rose again with every step up to the glass-front store.

The sound of her keys against the door echoed in the

open space of the first floor studio. The tearing in her chest turned her stomach and rolled through her body. It was dark inside lit only by thin streams of morning sun. Cloth shrouded sculptures lined the walls like Halloween ghosts. No movement. No sound. Sarah looked at the ceiling as if she could see through the floor into the apartment above. She knew without justification that something was undeniably wrong.

"Daniel?" Sarah dropped her things inside the front door and took the first step up the stairs. "Daniel!" There was no answer. Two more steps. Silence. "If you've got someone up there you don't want me to meet, you better send them down the fire escape. I'm coming in!" She reached the landing in front of the apartment door without hearing a shuffle. "Daniel…" Quieter this time, and begging, "Daniel, please…" She closed her eyes and listened for his heartbeat, for a fleeting thought, anything at all across the connecting fibers of their minds. Nothing came. She turned the handle and fire exploded in her chest.

Sarah clamped her eyes shut within the same second that she saw her absolute worst fears were realized. The floor met her knees and she clung to the door handle, gasping for air. The understanding spread through her mind, pulling her closer and closer to the floor. Her chest erupted in searing, flowing pain.

TWO

Seconds turned into minutes as Sarah took only quick glances towards her brother. Daniel's legs splayed out in front of him, a smear tracing an arc away from a pitted gouge in the brick wall towards his body. Daniel, laying on his side, his left hand a fist around something white. His face propped against the bookcase at an unnatural angle where his slide down the wall was halted. She wanted to reach out and sweep back the long brown hair that cloaked his eyes but the blood stopped her. A thin dark trail led from a blackened hole in his bare chest to a slick crimson pool surrounding him. His right arm outstretched, palm down like an ivory bridge across a deep and glassy pond. A path that led to a revolver hung around his index finger.

Stars burst blurring her vision and she remembered she needed to breathe. A deep breath brought in a rush of panic and the smell of blood. A new wave of nausea threatened to overtake her. Sarah retreated into herself to the place that only Daniel could access. She let herself slip inside, into her head and reached out to Daniel with her thoughts. Even in the silence of the last few weeks, she could still sense him. She repeated his name over and over, but it just echoed in the emptiness then, like a physical force shoving her from that secret corner, blackness closed in and she was looking at the floor again.

She retrieved her cell phone from her pocket with shaking hands.

"911, what is your emergency," said a voice on the other end of the line.

"My brother... he's been shot..." Sarah could barely speak.

"Ma'am, are you in a safe place? Is the shooter still nearby?"

"I don't think anyone's here."

"What's the address, ma'am? I'll have the police and an ambulance dispatched right away."

"214 South E Street."

"Stay on the line with me, ma'am. What's your name?"

"Sarah."

"Where are you in the building, Sarah? Will the police be able to get in?"

"I'm coming out. I locked the door when I got here."

Sarah climbed down the stairs, unlocked the front door and stepped out into the icy morning light. The pain that had been plaguing her since the night before made sense now. She could feel in her chest where the bullet had passed through his heart. Sarah had known. She'd known something was wrong since the first pang in her stomach. Just like she'd known when Daniel fell off his bike in Central Park and sprained his ankle when they were eight or so many other examples throughout their thirty years when the other just knew. Yes, she had known. Her stomach turned again and this time, falling to her knees, the nausea couldn't be held back. She stayed stooped over the curb in case of another attack. The sound of sirens grew closer and closer. Soon, a whirlwind of officers and paramedics surrounded her, passing by on every side. She could hear the policemen banging open doors shouting "clear" back and forth between them.

Four cops? Five? She couldn't tell. She had the vague impression that someone was talking to her, but all she could feel was the icy ground tearing into her palms and knees and the flaming stabbing wound through her heart.

There were hands on her, lifting her to a standing position and guiding her somewhere. She refused to open her eyes to see or to care. Focused on breathing, she kept her eyes shut as if keeping them closed could negate what she had seen.

Sarah counted off seconds during an inhale then was distracted by the sound of another siren blaring vehicle approaching. The metallic clatter of what she assumed was a stretcher passed by. The dizziness returned. She realized that she was holding her breath and forced an exhale then fought for another inhale. The cold air calmed the nausea. She breathed out and took in another breath. Over and over she gasped, pausing a little too long after each exhale. The darkness behind her eyelids deepened, her limbs grew heavy then consciousness left her to crumple towards the ground.

SARAH COULD HEAR a voice she didn't recognize coming from the far end of a very long tunnel. She closed her eyes tighter; it was too early to wake up, surely. Against her will, her arms and legs began their signals to her brain and she became more and more aware that she was not in her bed at home.

"Sarah? Sarah, can you hear me?"

Sarah allowed her left eye to crack open enough to see the paramedic before her. A weak "yeah," was all she could muster.

She opened her eyes in earnest this time and immediately wished she hadn't. From the front door came two paramedics guiding a stretcher towards an ambulance parked further down the sidewalk. Any hope that may have been lurking in her heart was now dashed at the site of the zipped black bag that could only contain Daniel's body. The paramedic with his hand still on her shoulder did a slight sidestep in an attempt to block her view of her dead brother's recessional.

Sarah tried to stand up, but the paramedic held her fast. She was too weak to protest, and suddenly, she was very cold. Instinctively she clawed at where her coat should have been, but of course it wasn't there. She tried to remember what happened to it as the paramedic pulled a wool blanket around her shoulders. She held on to the edges of the blanket and wrapped herself as tight as her weakened arms would allow. The paramedic was still talking, but she couldn't make out the words. She shut her eyes again.

SARAH FLOATED CLOSE enough to the surface of awareness to hear the paramedic arguing with an officer.

"She can't be questioned! She's barely conscious! We need to get her off the sidewalk and take her to the hospital."

"No!" Sarah's eyes flew open. "I don't need to go to the hospital."

In a panicked effort to prove her strength, she slipped out of the wool cocoon and stood. The crunch of the ice beneath her feet startled her and the chill that struck her made her instantly regret the loss of the blanket. She forced her knees to remain steady and braced herself against another wave of nausea threatening to overtake her. She swallowed hard and took a step towards the officer.

"You need to ask me some questions?"

"I'm going to get your coat for you. It'll be much warmer

for us to talk at the station if you feel up to it. We just have some questions to ask and we can help you make the necessary phone calls."

"That's fine."

She saw the officer's face for the first time. He was only an inch or two taller than Sarah, and couldn't be much older. She searched his features wondering if she recognized him; his short blonde hair peeking out from underneath his hat shielded a nice face, even as there was an odd look in his blue eyes. Sadness? Fear? She couldn't tell.

The paramedic's hand was back on her shoulder. He looked like the police officer. She wondered if they were brothers. The thought sent an electric surge of agony through her bones, but she willed herself not to flinch.

"Are you sure? You don't have to talk to them right now. You can take your time you know. I mean, you were just unconscious." His concern allowed a twinge of comfort. Part of her wanted to climb into an ambulance and lock the doors to escape.

"I'm okay, but thanks." She tried for a smile, but she wasn't sure that her face moved at all. The officer returned with her coat. Slipping it on mindlessly, she allowed herself to be led to one of the nearby squad cars.

"Will someone lock up? They don't have the keys," she asked the officer as she settled into the front seat.

"Don't worry. We'll handle all that."

It didn't answer the question which was uppermost, but at that exact moment maybe nothing could.

THE POLICE STATION was stifling compared to the frigid air outdoors. Despite the rising temperature, Sarah left her coat on, even going so far as to pull the dark wool more tightly around her. It was the only thing holding her in one piece.

Who do you call? Sarah's mind spun sitting alone with her cell phone and a cup of black coffee. Scrolling through her contacts she settled on her lawyer. She flashed to another time when she made the same call to him from a very similar waiting room. It struck her that the only person left in the world on which she could rely was a person she paid to be reliable.

"Clark Sterling," he answered.

"Clark, it's Sarah."

"Sarah! Merry Christmas, dear. How's…"

"It's Daniel," she interrupted. "Daniel is… Well, I'm at the White Plains police department. I'm going to need some help."

"What for this time?"

"Clark… he's gone."

"Missing?" Her silence struck a chord in him. "I'm walking out the door right now, Sarah. Sit tight." The line went dead.

"Ma'am? I'm Detective Spencer. I just have a few

questions." He held out his hand so she set down her phone and shook. Unbuttoning his brown polyester suit jacket, his overgrown salt and pepper mustache displaying his age, he took a seat opposite her and laid an open note pad on the table before him.

Sarah had to clear her throat just to manage an "okay." She answered the questions the officer had, when did she arrive, what did she touch, move, see?

"When did you last see Daniel?"

"Thanksgiving."

"Where was that?"

"His place here in White Plains. We were supposed to go to out of town but..." her voice and focus trailed away.

"Why did you change plans?"

"Daniel was going to propose to the person he was seeing so he didn't want to leave."

"What's his girlfriend's name?"

"Boyfriend. His name is Sam Jones. And they aren't together anymore."

"Sam said no?"

Sarah only nodded. That had been the day Daniel became silent in her mind.

"How was Daniel dealing with that?"

"Not great, but he was working through it. He's been keeping himself busy with his sculptures."

"Was he in any trouble? Any drugs or anything?"

"He's had problems with pain killers from time to time. Ever since a car accident we were in 12 years ago."

Something changed in the detective's manner, "Did you know Daniel had a gun?"

"No... I don't know where that came from."

"Okay, well, I'm going to need you to hang tight for a while. Do you have some family or a friend that can come and sit with you?"

"I have someone on their way."

"I'll check on you in a while." Detective Spencer and his note pad left the room.

Pulling her coat tighter against her chest, Sarah laid her head down on the cool laminate tabletop and replayed the image of the gun.

HER EYES SHOT open with the creak of the door. She didn't know how much time had passed since her cheek touched the table. Clark Sterling stood in the doorway, his gray pinstripe suit pristine and dark hair just as perfectly tailored. Sarah saw him the first time when she was 16 and him the new 28-year-old hotshot lawyer for her father's company. 14 years may have passed but he still conveyed the same imposing presence he did that first day.

Clark didn't so much talk to Sarah as he talked around her. He spoke to the police, called insurance companies, talked to the medical examiner's office, a funeral home, a cleaning crew. She only picked up words here and there, but she was grateful that someone else was doing all the doing. Breathing was enough to concentrate on. He asked her about people that needed to be notified and she slid her phone towards him. He went through her contacts one by one, and she either nodded to confirm or shook her head for him to move on. They skipped the majority making exception for a few old friends of their parents and her director at the publishing company.

Clark argued in the distance over the status of her luggage currently quarantined at what the police were calling a crime scene. Whispers fluttered around her of suicide and gunshots while sidelong glances offered pity one moment and accusation in another. Every time she tried to form a thought all that would come was an echoed, *Daniel, where are you? Daniel, what happened?* Her questions bounced back unanswered, so she focused on not thinking at all.

Sarah was ushered by Clark into an empty room without any awareness of her own movement. The only softness present in the sterile, tobacco-tinted room was a past-its-prime leather sofa and two club chairs. It's a shrink's office from the '70s, she thought.

"Sarah, I need you to focus for a minute."

"Huh?" The warm grip of his hands on her shoulders lured her back to the present.

"I need to go finish up with the police. We'll figure out

what's going on. It's best you stay put until I come for you, okay?"

Sarah simply nodded. He'd given her very similar instructions over a decade ago. Memories flashed like sharp daggers and she cringed away from them.

"I'm going to tell them to keep everyone out. Is that what you want, Sarah?"

"Did anyone answer the phone?" Sarah wondered all of a sudden. "When you called people, did anyone answer?"

"It's still very early, Sarah. They'll call back and I'll handle it. Do you want me to tell them where you are?"

"No. Keep my phone, okay? I think I'm going to lie down for a minute." She was becoming more lucid and she didn't like it.

"That sounds good, Sarah. I'll just be down the hall."

"Clark?"

"Yes."

"Thanks for coming so quickly."

"Try to rest, Sarah," he swept her bangs out of her eyes then pulled his hand away just as quickly. "I'll take care of this."

It felt strange to refer to what had transpired during the early morning hours as "this," but she resolved it was as good a word as any. She certainly couldn't define what happened and she refused to try to process it now. Sarah firmly clamped shut the part of her mind where Daniel usually entered so she would no longer be haunted by the constant echo. That place was empty now and she felt only the broken places of her heart. She sank into a corner of the couch and let her head rest on the well-worn arm. The growing fog enveloped her.

THREE

A VOICE TUGGED SARAH from deep sleep. Slowly, the room came into view and a sense of panic invaded her.

"Sarah, its Clark. Sorry to wake you."

"It doesn't matter."

"I've got to talk to you about a few things."

"Of course." A sudden realization hit her. "Clark! It's Christmas Eve! You shouldn't be here. You shouldn't be dealing with this now!"

"Don't worry, this is what I do." He held out a Starbucks red cup and caught her eye. She glanced away as quickly as she took the cup, afraid to see the compassion or pity or whatever his eyes were filled with.

"Thanks for that," she said, raising the cup in a slight toast. She wished it were a bottle of gin and the taste flashed across her memory as a whisper that she promptly shook off.

Clark could see the tension and fatigue in her eyes as if she'd aged 10 years in just hours. He dragged one of the two chairs closer to where Sarah remained on the couch. She noticed the fading daylight outside her window and felt guilty again for keeping Clark from his family then a new guilt took over for sleeping at all after what had been done to her brother.

"Okay, the police are doing an investigation, but with the holidays, it'll take a while. I've been assured that they will provide me with a list of anything removed from the house and I'll be notified when we've got the okay to send a cleaning crew." He flipped through several documents as he spoke, never looking up. "An autopsy is needed so that will be performed shortly."

"Do they have any suspects?"

"Not at the moment." She could feel his eyes on her again, "Sarah, I've got to tell you, they are not at all sure it was murder."

"Not murder? But…" She refused to vocalize the alternative.

"They are investigating, Sarah, but they say… they say it looks more and more like suicide."

"But how? How? You can't shoot yourself through the heart!"

"Sarah," Clark met her eyes, drew his right hand into a gun and pointed it at his heart, "you can."

"No," she shook her head and felt her eyes fill. He couldn't have done that without her knowing. She would have seen. The image of the revolver strung upon his index finger like a ring replayed itself but Sarah tossed it away just as quickly.

"There is nothing you can do about any of this now. I have your luggage. Why don't you let me take you back to the city?"

"I want to see him." Sarah did her best to steady her voice.

"I don't know…" Clark shook his head for the 'no' he really wanted to say. She knew why he didn't want her to see the body.

"I know it's bad, Clark. I don't care. I have to."

"I'll arrange it, but it's not going to happen for a few days at least." He leaned closer to her, his voice falling into the intimate tone that they'd both decided couldn't happen anymore. "Come on. Let me drive you back to the city."

"I'm fine, really." She met his eyes and instantly regretted it. He managed to make her feel protected and exposed at the same time.

"No, you're not." He rested a knowing hand on her shoulder. She finally nodded in silent assent. "That's settled then. Your bags are already in my car. Let's get you out of here."

Clark took her coffee cup as she stood up and rearranged her coat then handed it back as he ushered her out of the room and through the hallway toward the exit. She could feel silent glances as she passed. The touch of his hand on her back lingered until they were outside and he was opening the passenger door.

They'd never been big on conversation, even during the eight months they'd given "something more" a try, so she fell under the hypnotism of the sound of tires on salty roads. In the small familiar world of his black Audi, with the scent of his cologne mixing with the steam from the hot coffee between her two hands, she wanted to cut out the visions from the day and drive with him forever. The city instead encroached on her escape plan, and frantic thoughts burst forth as she tried to build out some semblance of a next step.

"Just let me out here."

"Sarah, it's just another street up."

"It's fine, I need the air."

He glanced her way, disapproving, but pulled up to the curb, popped the trunk, then got out to get her luggage. She'd almost forgotten how cold it was when the icy drafts hit her.

"I'll walk with you."

"No, you need to go. Tell the wife and kids I'm sorry I stole you away."

A sad stare filled the space where they may have embraced. Clark broke the silence, "I'll call you."

Sarah turned and walked away and quickly rounded the corner only slowing once she knew he could no longer see her. He'd dropped her off on that corner dozens of times and a map of these streets was burned in her mind, but still she had to get her bearings.

The rumble of the city that used to morph into white noise was now loud and caustic. It hurt her ears, her head ached and her heart pounded as if each honk of the taxi horns injected her with a shot of adrenaline. The anonymity of the city crowds once gave her the sense of comfort and belonging. Now she felt like a loose plastic bag buffeted by the rough wind tunnels stirred up by the skyscrapers. It wasn't until the doors to her apartment building closed behind her that there was room enough to breathe. The sound of her boots on the white marble expanse sent echoes in every direction disrupted only by the six marble columns that flanked her path to the elevators. The volume contrast of the elevator music to the street noise left her ears muffled and ringing.

The elevator doors slid closed. The woman staring back at her from the slick metal reflection was unrecognizable. Older. Paler. A sepia version of herself.

The elevator opened and Sarah hesitated before taking a step. Nearly every time those doors opened before her, she felt how ridiculous it was that only one person inhabited an entire floor. Sarah walked into the main living room of the apartment. Things were as sterile as when she had left them that morning aside from the bags she'd just abandoned to topple over. The stark white reached across the marble floor and up the blank walls like a solid canvas that now bled out across the snow coated balcony that ran the length of the room. A walnut desk looked out over the balcony through the wall of windows and glass doors and a tufted leather sofa floated in the center of the room facing nothing in particular. Sarah stood for a long time staring through the window out into the blanket of gray sky.

Her mind was a stalled engine. Breathing seemed exhausting and although she tried, she couldn't get any thoughts to start flowing through her mind. If she tried too hard, all she would get were flashes of Daniel's lifeless body.

She shook herself away from thinking and set her mind on autopilot. She didn't know how to be strong now that she didn't have someone to be strong for. It was always easy to do what needed to be done if it was for Daniel. With Daniel, she didn't need anything else.

What am I doing? What do I do? The questions began pulsing through her veins.

She stared at a blank wall and it became a self-portrait. There was nothing left inside her. All she had ever been was Daniel's and he had no need for her now. Since birth, when one laughed, the other laughed; when one cried, the other cried; but when one died...they never dared to consider what would happen.

Turning on her laptop, she opened her email and did what she could to switch off the gears in her mind. There were dozens of emails to sort through, another dozen manuscripts waiting in a stack on the desk for the edits of her red pen.

Feeling like she was betraying Daniel but not knowing

anything else to do, she clicked open one of the dozen red pens poised and waiting in an old coffee mug and flipped open the first page of the top manuscript. She busied herself with the meaningless rambling of the cut-rate author, as remnant snowflakes melted slowly on the shoulders of the winter coat she still wore.

THE SUN ROSE over Central Park on Christmas morning, never quite breaking through the thick layer of clouds. Sarah felt the pain in her neck and contorted arm before she opened her eyes. She had fallen asleep with the red pen still poised and it had formed a dime-sized blot where she'd rested it all night. Her mind began to rattle off facts. *You fell asleep at your desk. Ugh, your body hurts. It's Christmas morning… it's Christmas… Daniel is gone.*

She bolted for the nearest bathroom, flipped the lid, and fell to her knees just in time. Crumpling to the floor, she focused on breathing and forced all thoughts away. The cool tile floor was strangely comforting. The last time she'd been in this bathroom, she'd been kneeling next to Daniel. Sarah had run through "his room" without thinking.

They'd had a pattern to their lives since both of their parents passed. Daniel devoted himself to friends and lovers, disappearing for months on end, only to be disappointed and come back to Sarah. This had been her only comfort when he was missing from her life; she knew he'd be back. She did her best to befriend those that flocked around Daniel but she had no real need to be around them. She did it for Daniel.

Daniel hadn't been to the apartment in months, preferring his place in White Plains over the pomp of the Central Park West building. He managed to make exceptions for special occasions though, and the bed had remained unmade since the last night he'd drank too much and missed his train back home. Sarah slept in the chair beside his bed so she could hold his hair back when he woke up to get sick. There were times when Daniel was drunk that he looked so much like their father, so much so that she could barely look at him for fear of waking old childhood fears. But then a smug grin or teary eyes would wash away the paternal resemblance and she wouldn't be scared anymore.

The room was sparse with only a bed, an overstuffed chair, and a nightstand. Nothing fancy, just functional like most of the apartment. She knew this was his space, but it was as if he'd barely left a footprint. If the bed were made, no one would ever know he'd been there.

Every thought of Daniel was like a fierce stab to her brain and the tug between fight or flight turned her into a zombie. All the effort not to think about Daniel was wearing her down, but it was the pain from the broken place inside that was so exhausting. If she lost focus for even a single second, her mind would turn instinctively to that place where they could sense each other. Now, there was nothing.

She pulled the single framed black and white photo of the two of them from the nightstand and stared at his sweet smiling face. There was a pain behind his eyes, and for a moment, staring into his eyes, she could almost feel him. She was teetering as close to the edge as possible, reaching out over a great chasm, and barely brushing against his presence with her fingertips. In that moment, as she stared into his two-dimensional grayed out eyes, he was with her. His laugh echoed for just a fragment of a second. Then as the moment faded, the pain returned, and her eyes grew heavier.

Sarah walked through the rooms gathering the few framed photos they had and maneuvered onto the couch. Staring at the same photo of Daniel from before did nothing. She focused until her eyes burned from not blinking. She tried the picture of them as babies from her nightstand, but nothing came. She reached for the third.

The family in the picture frame stared back at her and tears stung her dry eyes. A smile tugged the corners of her mouth into compliance as she looked into the sunburned yet beaming faces of the 10-year-old twin boy and girl, their mother and father standing behind them resting their hands on the shoulders of their children. The little girl had the same eyes as Sarah and a matching crooked grin; it was hard for her to believe she had ever been that young. Daniel and Sarah looked so alike back then. He started growing out his hair after that summer in an effort to make them look even more identical. Sarah always seemed to wear his clothes out of detest for the frilly dresses their mother bought in hopes of making her a lady. The summer they turned 12, though, their attempts at being mirror images were permanently foiled with the emergence of Sarah's breasts. Daniel still teased that she had ruined everything; to this, she always replied that they had more than enough money to buy him a nice set to match.

The happy family in the photo was standing at the end of their dock with Lake Geneva behind them, nothing but crystal blue skies mirrored in the glassy surface. With her eyes closed, Sarah pictured that day. The camera in front of them precariously perched atop a stack of life vests on a fold up chair. Peering through the tree line, she could make out the front porch of their cabin. A fire was already lit in the fire pit on the beach. Daniel was squeezing her hand in anticipation of the s'mores they'd be gorging on as soon as the picture took.

Sarah's bare feet absorbed the warmth of the sun beaten wood beams below her and she felt alive. It was the first full day at the cabin for the summer and Daniel and Sarah would have three months to enjoy their favorite place in the entire world. Things were always better at the cabin, even their father seemed weightless and so the happy family existed again, if only for those few summer months.

At 10, they hadn't seen anything of the world except New York City, Geneva, Vermont, and the few things to see in between. At 30, after putting in their best efforts to be categorized as "world travelers" and with dozens of passport stamps as proof, Daniel and Sarah still made a pilgrimage to the family's cabin on the lake each summer and nearly every holiday. The most important events were never spent apart from the cabin or each other, holidays like Christmas, their birthday... the day their parents died.

Sarah gave the last photo one long stare then turned it face down on the cushion beside her and looked around the living room. This place didn't hold any real parts of Daniel. She needed to know what happened to him. She tried to rerun every word Clark and the police said, but only one word kept surfacing. *Suicide. No.*

People know Daniel has money; it could have been a robbery. She went on like this, grasping for straws, not knowing how she could possibly just sit and wait until someone decided to call her.

Christmas. Even New York slowed down for Christmas. Nothing could be done.

She wanted to fall back into the numbness of sleep, but couldn't shake the nagging sense of things needing to be done. Sarah stood and paced, drawing an outline of the room with her path. The first time back in the apartment after their parents died felt very much the same way.

The Central Park West apartment was a constant pet project of their mother's. Nearly every summer, while the family of four spent several warm months at the lake house, hoards of contractors and decorators would lay prey to the exorbitant square footage and remodel the entire apartment.

After the accident, Daniel and Sarah returned to a completely stripped apartment. It was as if their parents' presence had literally been ripped away from the space. Without any desire to spend time decorating and not really wanting to keep the apartment anyways, Sarah asked the contractors to just finish the space with white walls.

All the furniture and belongings that had been sent to storage during the remodel were delivered one morning, and not knowing what to do with it all, Daniel had the movers stack it floor to ceiling in the master bedroom. He locked the door and nailed the key to an exposed stud in the wall before the new drywall was installed and covered it up. They had never, in 12 years, cared to open that room although Sarah found herself touching the spot in the wall where the key was entombed as she walked down the hall from time to time. In hindsight, she wished they had simply sent all their parents' things to auction.

Initially, Daniel and Sarah lived like campers with air mattresses on the living room floor. The huge floor to ceiling windows facing out across Central Park afforded them a nice sky view of the stars and they would pretend they were back at the cabin.

Slowly, they accumulated a few furnishings and eventually

moved into bedrooms, but there were still more empty rooms than ones lived in. The all-encompassing white seemed to comfort them as if it gave their mind a break from trying to work out their surroundings. There was nothing to analyze, stir up memories, or complicate things when staring at white walls.

It wasn't that they didn't miss their parents, but they didn't need to talk about it to know what the other was feeling. They kept only a single framed family picture on the desk in the living room. A reminder of happier days with their parents, before things got complicated. The way they died… neither of them could shake the guilt for very long.

If I'd kept my mouth shut. If we'd just run away. Daniel's words bubbled up from the past and that old pain returned.

Sarah's memories ran back to their 22nd birthday, sitting motionless on a park bench, next to Daniel, overlooking the Pond and Gapstow Bridge. Her heart began to beat in slow motion and her body grew cold. His eyes were the last things she saw before she closed her own, sending one last tear down her cheek, his hand held hers and she was glad to be free.

Then there were sirens and someone yelling, "What did you take? What did you take?"

Daniel was kneeling beside her, his voice weak but he was still strong enough to dial 911 when Sarah lost consciousness. "The bottle is in my pocket. We both took 22. Don't let her die."

Three-days in the hospital under psych eval rounded out with 12 months of therapy and the twins passed as healthy twenty-somethings again. "Survivor's guilt" the doctors called it. They would never speak of that night again.

FOUR

EYES CAST CURIOUS glances laced with a hint of pity as Sarah waded through the vast sea of cubicles towards her office the following morning. There was no eye contact, though, and she was glad that no one said much to her. The last thing she wanted to hear was a vast showering of "I'm so sorry for your loss" and empty questions like "are you okay?" and "is there anything I can do?" Her stomach dropped when she opened the door to her office to find several obnoxiously huge flower arrangements adorning her desk.

"Miss Sarah?" A rhythmic clicking from heels on hard wood trailed close behind her. Sarah dropped her bag on the corner of her desk. "Miss Sarah, *what* are you doing here today?" Sarah didn't have to look up. The ridiculous spike heels and southern drawl gave her overly perky assistant away.

"Thanks, Marie Claire," Sarah still thought the girl had

lied about her name on her resume though she did look like she belong on the cover of a fashion magazine. "What does my calendar look like today?"

"Well, it's clear, ma'am. No one expected to see you for a few days at least."

"All right. Can you help me move these flowers? Maybe you'd like a few for your desk?"

"Of course, Miss Sarah." Marie Claire shifted arrangements to the side tables flanking a seating area while Sarah settled behind her desk and docked her laptop. She opened her inbox and found nothing new since the emails she attended to the day before. Her calendar was in fact clear for the entire week. Marie Claire set a steaming cup of coffee on its usual coaster, set a few pieces of mail into her inbox and tiptoed out of the office.

Sarah quickly sorted through the envelopes: a couple Christmas cards, a magazine she promptly tossed in the over flowing "to read" basket and a proposal letter that she added to the even taller stack in the "unsolicited" bin.

An 8:15 reminder popped up instructing her to take her vitamins. *Have I really only been here for 15 minutes?* She pressed the intercom button.

"Marie Claire, could you come in here please?" The girl was in the office before Sarah hung up the phone. "Please take all this unsolicited mail to the new junior editor. What's his name again?"

"Thomas."

"Right, let's see if he can pull a gem out of this mess. Here are a few manuscripts I'm finished with, just type up cover letters for me so we can get them in the mail?"

"Of course, Miss Sarah…. Um, Miss Sarah?"

"Yes."

"Thank you for the Christmas gift. I've never had a Louis Vuitton that wasn't bought off the back of the truck, if you know what I'm sayin'." A laugh escaped Sarah even though it sounded more like a cough.

"How do you know where I got it?" she winked at Marie Claire whose eyes finally looked a little less on edge. "You're very welcome. I hope you know I appreciate all your hard work."

"Thanks, Miss Sarah." Marie Clair drew a circle in the carpet with the toe of one sure, "I'm sure everyone is asking so I'm sorry but are you okay?"

Sarah met the girl's eyes and, for the first time, saw an actual friend in Marie Claire.

"Honestly, I don't know. But busy seems to help so I'm here."

"I get it. Just let me know what I can do." Marie Claire gave her a sad grin. "I mean it, anything," as she backed out of the office, weighed down by a foot and a half of stacked paper.

Sarah swiveled in her chair to face the view from her window, coffee cup in hand. Another gray day. A drizzling rain was melting snow into slush that was now far from its newly fallen pristine sheen. The sidewalks were tiled with umbrellas, mostly black, but every so often a polka dot or a bright red streaked through.

"Miss Sarah?" Marie Claire's voice echoed through the phone's speaker.

"Yes?"

"Miss Celeste would like to see you."

"All right, I'm on my way."

Sarah couldn't decide if she wanted to talk to "Miss Celeste" or run the other way, but she made her way swiftly across the floor to the Editorial Director's office.

"Mrs. Delaney is expecting you. Please go in." Sarah tried to imagine Marie Claire addressing people with the same level of formality, shook away the absurd thought, and pushed open the door.

"Sarah!" Celeste had her in an embrace before Sarah could even focus on her face. "How are you, dear?"

"I'm… I'm okay, I guess." Celeste was a total Jackie O, complete with impeccable taste and pearl necklace.

"Sit down! Sit down!" Sarah obeyed and sat on one side of a white leather sofa, strewn with jewel tone velvet pillows.

"I'm so sorry, my dear! It's a tragedy, that's what it is… Let's talk about your plans, sweetie. How much time do you want to take off?" She took the tea cup Celeste presented, and surveyed the line of framed pictures lining the coffee table.

A photo of Celeste and Sarah's mother in cap and gown for their college graduation stood out prominently.

"Um, well, I'll have to take some time to wrap up things once the police figure things out, but that's as far as I can really plan right now."

"Sarah. Sarah, look at me." Sarah shifted uncomfortably in her chair but conceded to make eye contact. "You need to take some time off, okay? I know you too well. You can't just sweep this under the rug and go on with things."

"Celeste, I can do my job. For heaven's sake, it's just going to stress me out more to come back to a huge backlog after twiddling my thumbs in my apartment for a week or two. I've got to keep busy."

"You lost *Daniel,* Sarah…"

"Trust me, I'm aware. Very aware."

"No, listen. I've known you for too long, Sarah. I know what you went through after your parents passed. I was there, remember? You can't just 'carry on' like nothing happened."

"What are you trying to say, Celeste? It sounds like you're trying to let me go. I thought you were happy with my work here."

"Don't be silly. I would have let you go years ago if you weren't good at your job. Hell, Sarah, you turn the lights on in the place and you are here after the vacuuming is done. You are also the only senior editor that still does her own copy work. You are a gold mine, okay? Your ability to do your job isn't the issue here. I'm worried about *you*."

Sarah wanted to argue, but she knew there was truth in what Celeste said. After their parents' accident, Daniel and Sarah went through the motions of the funeral and legal meetings galore then the day after their parents were in the ground, they started college. It was expected of them, a rational next step when they had no other direction in the world. Was she doing the same thing now?

"I'm not trying to be mean, Sarah, but I really think its best." Celeste's eyes were tired yet kind. "You think about it and let me know, okay?"

"Sure," Sarah stood and made her way to the door. "Thanks, Celeste."

"You got it."

Sarah wove through the cubicle-lined pathways back to her office and was still a few yards away when an excitable squeal from Marie Claire bridged the distance.

"Oh good! You're back. I was just about to hang up. Mister Clark is on the line. Shall I put him through?"

"Yes, thank you... maybe no more caffeine for you today, okay?"

Sarah closed the door behind her with Marie Claire still giggling. Her heart took pace with the rapidly blinking line on the telephone. *Do I really want to hear anything he has to say?* Even if the police found something, it wouldn't make anything better.

"This is Sarah," she said after ripping the phone from its holder like a Band-Aid over a tender spot.

"Sarah, it's Clark. How are you doing?"

"I'm fine."

"You didn't answer your cell… I thought you might be at the office."

"You found me," she was getting annoyed at the pregnant pauses. "What's going on? Is there news?"

"Yeah, I… I didn't want to do this over the phone…"

She cut him off, "Clark, I've been waiting, just tell me."

"All right, the police just notified me that they're finishing up. The autopsy was completed first thing this morning and they are ready to close the case."

"Close the case?"

"Sarah… why don't I head over there? I can be there in 15 minutes."

"Spit it out Clark! What the hell happened!?"

"Well, it's what we thought it was… the cops wanted to be certain because of where the gunshot was, but…"

"Are you trying to tell me my brother did this to himself?" His silence answered. "*No, Clark! This is all wrong!*" The searing pain in her chest that she'd been keeping at bay burst over the levies and the walls began to spin in her vision.

"Sarah, breathe."

She heeded the command and the speed of the spinning walls slowed to a crawl. As she surrendered herself to the chair,

"Was there even a note?"

"Yeah. Yeah, there was a note. Look, I'm going to go ahead and move forward with getting cleaners into the apartment."

"Good," she said after a long pause. "Can we just get all the paperwork out of the way? You know how much I hate legal crap."

"Sure, I thought you'd say that so I cleared my schedule."

"I'll be there soon."

"Let me send a car for you."

"Fine." She didn't have it left in her to argue.

They are wrong. I would have known. They're wrong. They're wrong. Daniel? What happened to you? She searched inside for even a wisp of their connection, but found nothing. *Damn it, Daniel! Talk to me!* She clenched her eyes tighter and tighter, holding her breath in desperation only to slam up against the solid walls of the empty chamber inside where her sobs echoed.

"Miss Sarah?" The voice jolted her back to the office and toward the intercom.

"Yes." Sarah smeared away tears she hadn't realized were streaming down her cheeks.

"I'm going to get more coffee. You want me to bring you something back?"

"No thank you, I'm going to leave in just a little while."

"Okay. You just call if you need any single thing, all right?"

"All right."

Sarah picked up the phone and dialed. "Celeste? It's Sarah."

"Sarah, is everything all right?"

"Yes… no… I… you're right. I think I need to get out of town for a while."

"I understand, dear. Take all the time you need."

"I'll have Marie Claire send things on to me…"

"Sarah, stop. We'll manage. You focus on you, okay? You're already in enough pain I don't want you dealing with the wannabe literary fiction novels from a bunch of NaNo speed writers. If Mr. King decides to grace us with something, I'll call you."

"Thanks, Celeste."

"You got it."

THE CITY WAS cold and unforgiving. The grays of the sidewalks and buildings seemed to seep into her bones and drag her deeper into the pale numbness consuming her mind. She reached the attorney's building and flowed into the nearest elevator with the pack of matching suits going about their day. At the 25th floor the doors parted revealing a lobby of neutral blandness. Sarah suspected it was meant to be soothing, but it instead made her think of dead leaves and melted chocolate ice cream cones.

"Sarah, he's all ready for you."

Is it strange that the receptionist at a law firm knows you by first name? Sarah thought, and then explained it away as a contrived attempt to make clients' visits feel more personal. She walked past the receptionist's desk down a hall to the double oak doors to Clark's office. The door was opened before she could touch the handle.

"Sarah…" He filled her name with more meaning than she cared to entertain. She knew his concern was genuine, but she was growing weary with attempting to discern intentions. "I've sent for some coffee… this may take a little while, but I think we'll have everything squared away after we're finished."

She took a seat on the sofa, tucking away unnecessary overstuffed chenille throw pillows, and was reminded of the most recent time she'd given therapy a try… it had been a very short lived venture.

A knock at the door signaled the entrance of a green-as-they-come intern, immaculately kept hair and starched white shirt with a slightly off kilter tie that gave him away, and the coffee had arrived. It seemed interns were running the world. *Nothing quite like free labor. I wonder if the way I take my coffee is logged away in one of these files or if he actually remembered.*

"Okay, are you ready to start working through some of this?"

Sarah nodded, taking a sip of her coffee.

"Now Daniel's will is clear and his assets will fold into the family trust. You are already on the title and insurance for his truck, so that was transferred easily. I've prepared copies of the necessary documentation in this portfolio until the final versions are completed. All accruing expenses will be taken care of by the trust. He wished to be cremated, is that all right with you?"

"Um, yeah." She was grateful he didn't say Daniel's name. She didn't want to think about for whom she was making unalterable decisions.

"You'll need to meet with a funeral director."

"No. No funeral. I know he didn't want a funeral."

"Well, it's really for you, Sarah."

"I don't need it."

"Okay, so it's not just for you. He was a respected member of the community. You should really think of at least holding a memorial."

"I'll think about it," she conceded, mostly to ward off the baffled look she was receiving.

They continued this way through the afternoon reviewing lists of family assets, inventories from Daniel's storage unit and apartment, revising the trust documents... pages and pages of legalese that Sarah could really care less about. *Strange,* she thought, *that a person's life can so easily be reduced to a short stack of legal documents.*

"Have you thought about what you want to do with the property?"

"What property?"

"Daniel's building."

"Sell it."

"Are you sure? It could prove quite profitable as a rental property."

"No, I don't want to keep thinking about it. It's better if we just sell it."

"Of course. As for the contents... would you like me to have them packed and moved to a storage unit?"

"No. Have it all moved to the apartment. I just want it all together. Just make sure they take extra care with his statues. I'll head to White Plains as soon as you say I can. I want to be the one to pack up his things."

"I understand. I'll make the arrangements with the movers."

"What about the things the cops have? I... I want the letter."

"When you get to White Plans you'll need to stop at the police station to sign for his effects. I had Daniel's truck parked at the police station so you'll need to get a cab from the train." He slid the keys across the desk towards her

"Okay. Good." She squeezed the keys in her hand in an effort to extract any last presence of her brother.

She left the office a million signatures later with a fat legal sized envelope in her hand, still not knowing what to do past remembering to breathe.

FIVE

As DANIEL'S TRUCK rounded the side of the police station, Sarah held her breath. She had not anticipated the surge of pain. The officer held the driver's side door open for her and she pulled out a few bills to tip him, delaying the moment when she would be inside the truck, but the officer smiled, shook his head and refused. He held the door for her. Sooner than she wanted, she was sitting in the driver's seat next to a box sealed with red evidence tape resting on passenger's side. The familiar first few notes of Daniel's favorite song pricked like needles and she just wasn't ready. She ejected it quickly slid the disc into the visor before Tom Petty could sing the first word, but the lyrics played on in her mind. *She wore faded jeans and soft black leather... her eyes so blue they looked like weather.* The last time she drove the truck, she'd borrowed it to find a store open Thanksgiving morning to buy dinner ingredients that Daniel had forgotten.

Sarah realized that she would never again be fixing dinner with Daniel. She couldn't breathe and with every second her heart seemed to threaten never to beat again. Sarah willed herself to inhale and concentrated on the snow piles on the sides of the road. Slowly she weaved through the streets, taking a circuitous route to Daniel's street. She pulled up to his building and sat with the engine running, trying to build up the strength to go inside.

Maybe this was all a bad dream and she would wake up to hear Daniel banging around in the kitchen. They would eat waffles and drink eggnog. He would open his gift from her and they'd plan a return to the lake house to make use of the new kayaks she bought for use in the warmer months. Then she remembered the two miniature kayaks wrapped in green paper still tucked into a sock in her suitcase. She had been sure she was going to stump him this year. They could always guess their presents to each other, but she really thought she had him.

Summoning up all the energy left in her body, Sarah pushed open the door and slid out onto the icy curb.

On the sidewalk beside the front door, flowers and candles had piled up. Car doors slammed behind her before she could examine the little shrine with much detail. She watched as the couple approached. The woman knelt to lay down a bunch of carnations.

"Did you know Daniel?" The man asked.

"Um, yeah. He's my brother."

"Oh my goodness! You're Sarah!" the woman shrieked, popping up from the sidewalk. Suddenly Sarah had the arms of a stranger wrapped around her. "I'm Karen! I'm sure Daniel's talked about me. I just arranged a showing of his work at The Exhibition. I can't believe this happened!"

Speech escaped Sarah.

"I'm Blaine. It's a shame to meet under these circumstances. Daniel always spoke so highly of you, I'm very sorry for your loss." The man held her hand in an extended handshake that was a little too long for Sarah's comfort.

"When is the funeral? We haven't heard a thing yet. I was sure there would be something in the paper, but the write up just said 'to be determined.'"

"Yeah, nothing has really been decided just yet."

"Well, his work? Can it still go up in the show?" The desperation rolled down her cheeks, but Sarah wasn't so sure sadness was in them.

"I…" Sarah was completely taken off guard.

"Karen, it's all right." Blaine reined her in with an arm around the shoulder.

"Sorry, I just…"

"No, Sarah, you don't need to worry about that right now."

"Thanks, um. I'm sure something can be arranged." Karen

was embracing her yet again before the couple returned to their car. The hugs seemed hollow and the sympathy didn't have time to soak in before it faded away.

The keys rattled from the shaking of her hand as she fumbled with the lock. She took a deep breath then pushed open the door. The room was long and narrow with windows along the front side facing the street. The ceiling was nearly 20 feet high in the front of the building where Daniel had installed sky lights, just so the front would be pooled in light from above. There was no light today. Sarah left the front doors wide open for light as she stepped further in from the front door. The rest of the first floor was open space wrapping around the spiral staircase in the center of the room and interrupted by a few columns that supported the second floor. The other three walls were exposed brick covered in patches by remnants of chipping plaster and holes where bolts used to be. Cloaked with white drop cloth that looked very much like ghosts along the walls were Daniel's statues.

Sarah noticed a larger covered sculpture in the center of the room. It hadn't been there the last time she'd visited and it was larger than all the rest. She neared it with a sense of anxiety that she couldn't pinpoint. Reaching out, she pulled off the canvas to uncover two figures standing side by side holding hands, their free hands placed over their hearts. Sarah found herself eye to eye with the life-size marble people who wore the two faces she recognized so well. They were a mirror of Daniel and her.

"We look so serene," she said out loud, "this is beautiful, Daniel." He had managed to indeed stump her with his gift this Christmas. Here it was, the only Daniel she'd be able to keep. She touched his face, traced his long carved hair. Was this how he wanted to be remembered? Turning her back to his cold face, she returned to the front doors and pulled them closed with frozen numb hands, throwing the room into a temporary darkness until her eyes adjusted.

Sarah had hoped that being in his space would help, that the fleeting sensation of him she felt for a microsecond while holding his photo the other day might return and, hopefully, it would be stronger. So far there was nothing; not even when up close to the work he was most passionate about. Sarah climbed the stairs to the apartment. The only thing that was making her brave enough to see the place where he'd died was the hope of finding the connection again.

As she opened the door, a vision of Daniel's slumped body flashed before her. She blinked it away to reveal a freshly painted wall opposite her. The cloying remnants of the latex scent stirred with wafts of Clorox and Murphy's Oil soap. These floors had never shined before as they did now. She wished she could crack open the plate glass windows to clear out the intoxicating mixture. The searing pain returned to her chest, throbbing as if bullets passed through repeatedly.

Sarah leaned back against the closed door and flipped

the light, trying to make the room look different. Something seemed to be missing, but she couldn't put her finger on what. On the dining table was a stack of flattened packing boxes left by the cleaning crew. She wished her methodical compulsive side would kick into autopilot, but it just wasn't showing up on cue. Wave upon wave of what could only be described as misery cast over her and stars flashed before her eyes... she'd forgotten to breathe again.

With all the forward momentum she could muster, she forced the first box into place and headed into the kitchen. It was subconscious that she opened the liquor cabinet first. One lone half consumed bottle of gin sat on the shelf. She knew she would do it before the cap was unscrewed, tossed into the trash can and the bottle tipped back, right into her waiting mouth.

The warmth spread down her throat into her stomach, filled her lungs and into her long deep breaths. Another swig later and the heat traveled down her arms; her face felt like the sun was beating down upon it. Sarah stood motionless except for the steady rhythmic movement of her arm carrying the bottle to and from her lips.

Her legs felt more and more like stretched out springs and she hated herself. She slid down the wall, ending up cross-legged on the cool and newly polished wood planks. She reached up and turned the light off.

She watched the time pass in slight shadows moving across

the floor. The wall of floor-to-ceiling frosted glass glowed eerily in some spots from lights and motion below. The sound of cars pulling up and leaving drifted, but she couldn't seem to move her eyes from the blank wall opposite her. The room seemed so empty. Daniel never collected much stuff, but she was sure things were missing. The bottle rolled away from her, singing its hollow echo, across the slightly slanting floors.

Her legs had thoroughly abandoned her so she crawled her way to Daniel's bed. Pulling the pillows over her head she pressed her face against them and inhaled. The scent of Daniel rushed into her head and lungs and the fire returned in her chest, but this time she didn't care. The world began to fade at the edges, and then turned black.

SARAH PUSHED HER way out of the pillow-made fortress, foraging for the memory of whose bed she was in and how she got there. No light shone through the glass walls now and the sounds of the street were missing. Sarah detangled herself from the sheet and crept back to the front door of the apartment. Opening the door slowly, she peeked out at the room below. She was alone. Very alone.

Returning to the kitchen, she pulled a glass from a cabinet and filled it from the tap. She glanced at the one assembled yet empty box at the other end of the counter. She pulled her phone from the security of her back pocket and texted Clark,

"I'm going to need you to arrange for Daniel's place to be packed up after all. Just taking a few things for now."

Somewhere between waking up and the first sip of water she knew she wouldn't be going back to New York any time soon. She had what she needed to work in her bag, but she'd need more clothes where she was going. She opened the closet and pulled out two old backpacks, patches sewn on from top to bottom from every country they'd stepped foot in. The first one was hers and was packed and ready with a week's worth of clothes in case of a spur of the moment trip to the lake. Returning to the closet with wide arms she pulled the section of t-shirts and sweaters, hangers and all, from the rail, noting the smell of his lingering cologne. She dumped them on the bed then, one by one, pulled out the hangers and tucked the shirts into Daniel's empty backpack. It was a lucky thing that, after all that time, Sarah still wore Daniel's clothes on a regular basis. She dug out her snow boots from amongst his many pairs of shoes, kicked off her Vans and laced up the boots. It wasn't until she was making her way out of the apartment that she saw Daniel's worn mustard yellow pea coat hanging from a hook near the door. She zipped the hoodie she was wearing and slipped on his coat over top.

Juggling the two bulging backpacks, she turned off the lights and locked the door behind her on the way to the truck, still parked in front of the building. Opening the passenger door, she flung the backpacks and her work bag on the floor board. Resting her eyes once again on the box in the seat, she felt compelled to secure it with the seatbelt as if it were a child. There was one more thing she had to do before heading out of town.

THE HOSPITAL WASN'T far away and she parked near the main entrance. The presence of Daniel's scent on the coat she now wore filled her with a longing to see her brother that helped overcome her fear. She could feel the distance between them drawing closer as a person in a lab coat led her down crisp white halls. She pushed away the image of Daniel's body behind a steel door in a sliding drawer; a filing cabinet for bodies. She shivered.

The medical examiner, putting on her best sympathetic face, led Sarah into a sterile room with only a table positioned in the center draped with a white sheet covering a human form. It struck her as she approached the cloaked figure, that the night before she had pulled back the curtain to an image of Daniel, and she reached out to do it again, half expecting to find a marble form laid out under the cover.

The sheet slid slowly, first revealing the brown of his hair, his forehead, eyebrows, and closed eyes. Sarah took a deep breath then with a surge, pulled the sheet back all the way to his waist. The ME, who had stood back, seemingly to give her space, rushed forward as if to stop her, but Sarah held up her hand.

"It's fine, I have to see it." As if studying the detail of the statue back in the studio, she traced the lines in his forehead, his eyebrows, his nose. He was, in fact, like marble. She stroked his hair and tears rolled down her cheeks and fell on his chest. The wound... the hole... she felt it burn in her own chest. It was comforting to know that she could at least still feel the pain even if everything else was gone. She hoped that the remaining pain meant she had pulled it all away from him as he died.

"Was it fast?"

The examiner came nearer again, "Yes. Yes, he passed quickly."

"Good." The tattoo over his heart caused a stinging sensation on the same place above her heart. Gemini symbols, the memory of the drunken night resulting in their matching tattoos made her smile and fresh tears poured. *We were supposed to take our final breath together.* She combed his hair with her fingers to frame his face and she fixed the sheet over his chest to hide the gaping wound, but still reveal the tattoo. He was a sculpture of himself sleeping. *Yes,* she thought, *he would have, in the end, carved himself.*

She stared for a long time without blinking, wanting to burn the peaceful image into her mind.

Daniel wasn't here anymore.

Her heartbeat echoed in her chest alone. Sarah bent and

kissed the cold forehead of the body that once held her other half as tears continued to fall from her eyes onto the gray eyelids below.

She'd always been able to sense him; they'd never been separated by more than a train ride. The hollow pounding of her heart told her he was much too far away now for her to feel him. She traced the tattoo and stared at the closed lids wishing to see the blue of his eyes one last time. With all the willpower she could summon, she turned and walked out the door, fighting every impulse to turn back.

Once in the empty hallway, an echoing sound made her realize she was sobbing. She steadied herself with an outstretched arm against the wall and took several deep breaths, wiping her eyes fiercely as if to punish them for giving into the weakness. With slightly more composure, she left the building, willing her body and her telltale red and puffy eyes invisible to any passerby.

S I X

FOUR LANE INTERSTATES gave way to two lane country roads rolling up and down progressively varying altitudes and through increasingly rural towns as Sarah drove from New York to Vermont. The last snow stuck showing that winter had set in and laid its roots for the next several months. The gray sky met the pristine white landscape in great contrast.

With the effort Sarah was expending to not think about anything, the static created in her mind distracted her until she recognized the exit for Burlington. The last "big" city before passing into the true wilderness of her destination, Burlington offered the last chance for extensive shopping. She cringed away from the familiarity of the Wal-Mart parking lot they'd always stopped at as she pulled in to stock up before making the last leg of the trip.

She filled her cart, navigating the aisles at a stroll with

no real timeframe or deadline for the first time in as long as she could remember. Firewood bundles and Duraflame logs, tortilla chips, coffee, ramen noodles amongst other trash food that made her cart load look like the spoils of a college freshman, newly free from the ordinance of parental dietary requirements. A feeling was developing inside that could only be described as mild uneasy giddiness, and she embraced the newness of this feeling over the ever present ache she so desperately sought to suppress. She let the temptations of the end caps catch her eye and ran her hands over a display of throw blankets until she found just the one she wanted to curl into and added it to the cart.

She shoved her now overflowing cart through the check-out lane and loaded the truck, all the more anxious to get to their happy place tucked away in the woods. She turned the truck onto an empty country lane that would take her the rest of the way to Geneva. Besides locals, no one made their way up to Geneva except the few campers and hikers that sought complete solitude, or wanted to smuggle things between the US/Canada border a handful of miles away.

The village of Geneva was small, only a few storefronts, cookie cutter church and steeple while most residences were scattered along the lake's edge. She was thankful for arriving on the outskirts just as the last light of the day faded. She hoped the truck could sneak through Main Street without being spotted. She pulled her knit hat a little farther down her forehead as she spotted Tom, the sheriff, postmaster and village gossip getting into his truck. He waved; surely recognizing the vintage Ford truck he'd helped Daniel restore a dozen summers ago.

In the complete darkness, finding the hidden driveway off the main unlit road was no easy feat and she had to creep slowly towards the dark cabin down the unplowed driveway to keep from getting stuck or driving off the edge. Pulling as close to the cabin as she could safely manage, she dug unsuccessfully through the glove box for a flashlight and resorted to lighting the way through foot deep snow with the LED light on Daniel's keychain.

As she climbed up the few steps to the porch of the cabin, memories came in flashes; Daniel napping on the hammock, Daniel piling wood, Daniel flinging the door open to greet her, Daniel racing through the trees to beat her to the lake... Daniel... Daniel...

What did you expect, Sarah?

She thought she would feel comforted, closer to him somehow, but the snapshots of Daniel only came when she closed her eyes. When she opened them again, it was just empty. Like someone de-saturated a photo; everything was less vibrant, all grays and browns now. Daniel made things come alive and without him, this place was dismal.

Pushing wide the front door of the cabin, a familiar scent met her and twinge of pain mixed with relief echoed through her body. Shaking herself to action, she flipped on the circuit breaker, wake the water heater, and turned lights on throughout the cabin. She made several trips back to the truck to lug in bags and the supplies, taking the sealed box directly into her bedroom and closing it in the empty armoire.

The familiar tasks of checking the fireplace flue and starting a fire kept her mind occupied and with the first warm crackles of the flame, she switched gears to unpacking. She took her time, doing her best not to focus on the details of the cabin and moved slowly putting things away in an effort to prolong the tedium. Her thoughts became a logical task list to which her body responded and began to relax. She shook out the new throw blanket, replacing the one purchased last year still draped across the arm of the couch. She neatly folded the older one and added it to a stack of similar blankets, counting out the number of winters they'd spent in the cabin.

As things fell into place and the room warmed, her mind, almost in fear of rising to the surface of reality, clouded over with overwhelming exhaustion. Determined not to waste the Duraflame log and too lazy to make a bed, Sarah pulled out several pillows and quilts from the chest under the window. She rooted around in Daniel's backpack until she touched the oldest and softest shirt, tugging it out to reveal gray cotton emblazoned with the Superman "S". She kicked off boots, hung Daniel's jacket on the back of a kitchen chair, pulled on the shirt and, turning off the lights, nesting into the couch.

She watched the light from the fire dance across the ceiling for what could only have been moments then she surrendered to sleep.

SILENCE. SARAH'S EYES fluttered open and realization began to form that morning had come. She lay motionless absorbing the quiet of the morning. From the window she could see the still bare branches of birch trees reaching toward the solid pale gray sky. She focused diligently on the qualities of the silence, noticing a humming in her ears at times and the slipping of ash in the fireplace. The chill in the room grazed her nose and cheeks so she broke her frozen position in order to pull the covers over her head and re-tuck her feet tightly. Leaving a small gap between quilt and pillow, Sarah watched the birch trees shiver with momentary breezes. Slowly, as the sky grew darker, her eyes grew heavier and sleep set in once more.

A GRUMBLING NOISE startled Sarah awake. Blinking hard, she grasped for memories of where she was and what day it was and what had woken her up. The growling came again and this time she realized it was her stomach. The icy air bit at her face and she instantly regretted letting the fire die out. Grudgingly she shoved the covers aside and, massaging out the crick in her neck and shaking blood back into a sleeping hand, she knelt to make a new fire.

The crackling sound was soothing as was the radiant heat that built until the whole log was aflame. Holding out her hands, she felt the waves of warmth roll over her fingers until they tingled. Slowly, her involuntary shivers subsided. Something was different. She twisted and bent at the waist, touching her toes. No pain. Sarah had lower back pain every morning since the car accident, baffling every doctor and chiropractor, since they could never find a reason. Daniel, on the other hand, suffered from spinal degeneration attributed to the accident. For the first time she connected the dots that the pain was always his, and now, like him, it was gone.

She distracted herself by making quick work of coffee and scrambled eggs while toasting bread. As her body came back to her, she allowed a few thoughts in, then instantly regretted them as a sudden ache in her stomach left her running for the bathroom.

She abandoned further ideas of food and instead brought her coffee to the small desk nestled under one of the windows facing the lake. Intending to check email or some other distraction, she turned instead to cleaning out the deleted and sent items. Nothing calmed her like empty folders. Her thumb slipped on the track pad and suddenly she was staring at an email she'd sent to Daniel over two years ago.

"Here are the first few pages... be kind," was all the email said. Before she could second guess herself, she opened the attached document. She read the words, knowing she'd written them, but feeling at the same time like they were altogether foreign. She'd long since deleted this file from her hard drive in her attempt to be "honest" with herself about the reality of her never becoming a real writer. It wasn't a coincidence, she was sure. It was Daniel, giving her this back.

She saved the file to her desktop and began reading again from the beginning. She pulled a pen from the top desk drawer and began her unconscious clicking on and off in the Morse code that used to make Daniel crazy.

SARAH SET HER pen down and stirred her coffee, resting her head on her other arm. She stared at the blinking cursor. Frustration did not capture what she felt. Four hours had passed since she settled at the computer to work yet nothing significant had come. Evening darkness would return soon. The sound of water lapping at the dock hung in the air. She wanted to drain the whole damn lake.

Coming here was a bad idea, she thought. Not once had she stayed here without Daniel. Being in their cabin by the lake only made the emptiness echo off the surrounding mountains. She thought the cabin would make him feel closer and that writing again, writing something that she'd started for him, would help her hear him again. She became more and more aware that she had died right alongside Daniel four days ago.

There was nothing left of her now. She was an empty shell.

Sarah stood with such force and frustration that the chair toppled over behind her. She pulled on Daniel's jacket, fastening each button up to her neck, tugged on her snow boots and marched out into the winter air without any plan or direction.

She only realized she'd walked out onto the dock when the sound of her boots hitting the ground changed from the crunching of iced over snow to the hollow clomping of boots on decking. Her knees gave out with little suggestion from her head, hitting the board below as the end of the dock came within a few feet. She stretched forward and settled on her stomach, crossing her arms at the edge as a resting place for her chin and hung her head over the ledge for the best view of the water. The still glassy surface reflected the sky as if it were an exact duplicate.

She expected to see Daniel in the reflection below... his face hanging over the edge just to her right, exactly where it ought to be. They had debated over what part of the earth they'd be if the choice was given. Daniel's answer changed from one day to the next. He would be the sky one day, the mountains the next, the ancient dead oak on the opposite bank on another. Sarah always chose the lake.

Daniel had always been this entire place: the air, the trees, the mountains. But the lake, well, the lake was just a mirage, a replica, a reflection of what it would never be. It only looked as beautiful as what it reflected and on this day, it was just an angry turbulent swirl of storm clouds. No, there was nothing beautiful about the lake, nor the tired, sad looking girl whose eyes stared right back up from the water's reflection.

Something dropped into the water just under Sarah and broke the serene surface into ever widening circle ripples. She hadn't realized she was crying until another hot tear rolled down her cheek and into the icy waters below. As if in response, a biting wind swept in, erasing the growing circles with hundreds of tiny dancing waves pushing to shore as if to say, "nothing more to see here."

SEVEN

FROM THE WARM comfort of the cabin the next day, Sarah stared at the lake and watched as the ice covering the water at the edges inched ever closer to the center. The ice hadn't yet reached the end of the long dock and water caught by the wind still lapped too loudly in the echoing silence. The sky in the distance looked ominous and having not planned well, she was running low on food and firewood. She didn't care much about the food, but she hated being cold so the firewood was essential, especially if the coming storm was as bad as the looming clouds indicated. She slid on Daniel's jacket, shoved her wallet in the back pocket of her jeans and wrapped an overly warm scarf around her neck twice before picking up the keys and a bulging envelope to mail back to the office and walked out the front door.

The trip into town was a short and familiar one. There

was one store that provided all the hardware, clothing, house wares, and grocery needs to the several dozen people living around Lake Geneva. Tom, the sheriff and postmaster, worked out of a building across the street and the resident hairdresser, who was also the local tavern keeper, kept shop next door. Sarah's return had not gone unnoticed but, as she pulled up in front of the general store, there was no one on the street to stare at her. For that, she was grateful.

Every sensation of this place flashed images of times gone by. The memories in the shop were cheerful ones though, and the sound of the bells hanging from the door handle brought back the taste of apple cider donuts. She inwardly grinned as she thought of the store keeper she had once been convinced was the real Santa Claus and who slipped candy into Daniel's and her hands when their parents looked in the other direction. Fred's booming voice preceded him as he made his way to the front of the store to meet her.

"Look who it is! I was wondering when you would surface. Knew you couldn't possibly make it long. Haven't had wood sent up to your place in ages!"

"Hi Fred," Sarah said with a pinched smile.

"You haven't been burning from that musty old wood pile, have you?" He teased.

"Well, I'm a bit of a traitor. I picked up a bundle from the Wal-Mart on my way up. Guess I forgot how quick it goes."

"Not to worry, not to worry," Fred chuckled. "Knew

you'd see sense and come a callin' with that nasty front moving in. Well, that and Tom had a big box come in for you today. Thought you'd come down to get it. I've already sent Jack up to your place with a cord of wood though; knew you needed it! You probably passed him on your way here." He was extremely pleased with himself and his jovial banter made Sarah feel safe. She'd missed Fred more than she knew and hearing his voice again felt like a character from a storybook coming to life.

A real smile escaped her and she quietly got out a "Thanks, Fred." He ushered her through the aisle filling up a box with food, candles and other necessities. She welcomed his friendly babbling on about the things that had changed in Geneva and the things that stayed the same. He ran through the short list of people who had moved away and the even shorter list of the people who had moved in.

She had lapsed into a bit of a trance focused on the rhythm of his words instead of their content and came to as Fred let out another hearty chuckle.

"Won't Beth be beside herself knowing she missed you! She'll be grilling me with details about how you look and how long you're stayin'. Well, I'll leave all that explaining up to you… I'm certain she won't let, but a day or two pass before she's knocking at your door with a half dozen pies, fresh baked, now that you've shown your face. None of us wanted to intrude, you know, but we've been waiting to see you, that's for sure."

They were back at her truck and Fred loaded the box of supplies onto the passenger seat. She did a quick search for her keys, patting down her jacket and pants in turn until she found them in her front jeans pocket. When she looked up, Fred was watching her. His smile had changed and there was an unmistakable hint of sadness in his eyes.

"I'm so sorry, Chipmunk. Don't you dare hesitate to call us if you need even one single thing." She tried to think of the last time Fred had called her "Chipmunk." She felt a pang of guilt. Fred and Beth were like grandparents to Daniel and her growing up and it had been too long since either one had seen them. For the last few years they'd just ducked in and out on short trips, not really making an effort to catch up with anyone from town. She felt even worse knowing that she should have been the one to tell them about Daniel, face-to-face, not letting them find out through the grapevine. Here Fred stood, and she was glad that he had known the Daniel she wanted to remember.

"Thanks, Fred. You tell Beth she better not drive up in this storm, but I expect pie very, very soon after." Sarah gave the best smile she could muster, but she felt her sorrow pull at the corners of her mouth. He understood and pulled her into the warmest bear hug since she'd been hugged by Daniel. The tension in her chest was welling up again and she looked forward to a good cry once she was alone again in the cabin.

"Now, you better run over to Tom's and get that box. You probably won't be pulling out of your driveway until the plow comes 'round."

"Aye, aye!" Sarah grabbed the envelope stuffed with the few manuscripts she'd completed and headed to Tom at the postmaster's office to get the rest of the work she'd sent for.

Marie Claire had been her usual frantic self, filling each breathy sentence with "Yes, Miss Sarah" than could ever be necessary. Sarah took ten minutes to convince her to pack up the work from her inbox and ship it to her since Celeste had insisted that Marie Claire not bother Sarah at all until she was back in the office.

A heavy glass door opened into the sheriff/post office. Tom sat behind the counter, teetering on the two back legs of his chair, sock feet propped on the tabletop and a portable TV complete with three foot long rabbit ears crackled through the evening weather report.

"Well, look who it is. I never know whether to arrest you or hand you your mail."

"Both are good options, but I'd prefer the mail just now."

"Ah Sarah! We were getting worried! Saw you pull through two days ago and I was just telling Doc Paul up the street that you were probably a Popsicle up there and we'd never know it."

"Sorry to ruin a good story there Tom, I've just been…"

"No need to explain," again with the sympathetic half

smile. "Well, we'd better get you out of here before the snow starts or you really will end up a Popsicle." Tom plopped a huge box on the counter and slid a clipboard her way. "Just sign here. You want me to take that envelope?"

"Oh, yeah. It's a paid envelope so it's ready to go." Sarah scratched her name in the "received by" column and slid the clipboard back towards Tom. "Guess I'll get moving then. Good to see you again, Tom."

"Good to see you too, kiddo. Once the storm blows through me and the wife'll be throwing a chili social, so we'll be expecting to see you."

"Sounds perfect."

The box was heavier than it looked and she nearly dropped it as she slid the last few feet back to her truck.

The drive back up the road to the cabin passed by so quickly that she could have convinced herself she hadn't left the house if it weren't for the new cord of wood stacked neatly on the side of the cabin. Sarah lugged the heavy box from the passenger seat and she staggered under its weight as well as its height blocking her vision. She was doing an odd side-step in order to see where she was going and regretting that she had waited until so late in the day to get supplies as the storm seemed to be kicking up the lake and blackening the sky. Reaching the porch, she balanced the box on a new neatly stacked pile of fresh firewood just outside the door as she fumbled with the doorknob.

The failing embers she had left in the grate had been stoked into a roaring fire in the fireplace. Sarah's city instincts made her panic for a moment. It had been a long time since she'd lived out here where you didn't lock your doors, and a fire waiting for you when you arrived home was a sign that a gentleman was thinking of the cold woman living in the woods alone. She fought back the alarm, knowing that Jack the delivery guy just did a kind deed. She did a quick search of the house, checking under beds and in closets for an intruder before making a mad dash back out to the truck to get the last box of supplies, then bolted the front door behind her.

She unloaded her purchases and made neat stacks on the desk from the contents of the box from Marie Claire. Determined to write something, anything at all, she brought her laptop closer to the fire and wrapped up in a thick blanket… then fell asleep at the first howling of the wind through the trees.

THE WHOLE NEXT day and night, the storm raged and so did Sarah's nightmares. She wove in and out of restless slumber, waking at times to see a few more inches of snow stacked up against the window.

The storm broke though, as a new morning rose and the sound of crackling fire and sizzling bacon woke Sarah. She imagined Daniel standing in the kitchen fighting to keep the temperature right and burning the bacon, dripping egg all over the counter and flour dusting the floor from an attempt at pancakes. He was hopeless, she thought, and smiled a little as she stretched and slowly opened her eyes.

As she looked around she realized the smell of bacon and fire were real and a grandmotherly figure stood with her back to Sarah in the kitchen, working away gracefully at the stove.

"Well, she lives!" Fred's familiar Santa-like voice came from the kitchen table. The sound of newspaper pages flipping and the welcome aroma of freshly brewed coffee wafted her way.

"Look at those eyes. My, my, my. Dear girl, have you slept at all? Well, I'll get you fixed right up," came the grandmotherly figure from the kitchen. "Coffee?"

Sarah nodded her head and blinked hard. This was a truly strange dream. She hadn't woken to breakfast in ages. Daniel tried once in a while, but was quite hopeless in the kitchen. The memory of the vision of Daniel she had as she stirred sent a twinge down her spine. This was nice though, waking to company... and to food. She thought she'd never want to see anyone, but having these two in her house, as if they were her very own grandparents, felt good... like family.

"Good morning," she said, not having to try very hard to give them a smile. "This is a surprise!"

"A good one, I hope," Fred said with his jolly chuckle.

"A very good surprise. I haven't had much of an appetite,

but waking up to Beth's bacon and pancakes... wow!"

"Well, get on over here to the table, dear. I've got some pancakes ready for you in just a sec."

With a mug of steaming coffee between her hands, she took in the room. Just having these two in the cabin made the place feel lighter and more alive. The sky outside was a bit brighter and the icy lake in the distance shimmered in the sunlight peeking through the clouds.

"So what have you been doing up here, Chipmunk?"

"Not too much. I thought I'd feel better here, but, well, the memories aren't enough, you know? I'm trying to write, but that laptop hasn't been doing much more than acting as a leg warmer."

"Give yourself some time, darlin'. And eat up! You're wasting away up here. We're going to have to stop in more often or you'll starve to death!"

"Well, I sure won't complain." And she meant it. This was nice. How could she have forgotten these people? It seemed like it had been so long since she'd felt cared for.

"I see Jack got you all set up with firewood."

"Yeah, he was nice enough to set up a stack at the door and had a fire going before I even made it home the other night."

"That Jack is a good boy. He's been working since spring to get that camp running again. Has a real work ethic, you know. You don't see that enough in kids your age."

Kids our age, she snickered inside. She may have taken offense to the comment if it had been from someone in the city, but coming from Fred, it felt loving.

"Wait, Jack? Little Jack from when we were kids? Wow, I haven't thought about him in forever. I didn't know his family still owned the place. That's great. If he gets it up and running again it'll be great for the village, I'm sure."

"Jack was glad to hear you were back in town. He was really upset when we told him about Daniel. I'd forgotten the three of you were pretty close back in the day. We are having him over for dinner tonight, you'd better join us. We're gonna watch the ball drop in Times Square."

"Oh, I don't want to impose," she said between bites of pancake.

"Nonsense. It's been too long since we've had young people around and it's good for us old folks. Keeps us on our toes. That and we've got to get some meat on those bones!"

"Well, all right, you don't have to twist my arm. I've forgotten what real food tastes like. This breakfast is amazing. Anytime you two want to drop by for an early morning wake up call, feel free."

"Early morning? Honey, it's two in the afternoon."

"Really?"

"Yes, ma'am. You'd better get yourself cleaned up and come on down to town for dinner at six. I have a feeling that caved in stomach of yours will be ready to eat again by then."

"You got it! Hey! How'd you get in anyway?"

"Chimney, of course."

"He's a comedian, this husband of mine. The hide-a-key is still under the bird feeder. When you didn't answer after we knocked three times, we got worried."

"I've been sleeping a lot... Huh, I didn't even know there was a hide-a-key."

The threesome chatted while she finished her meal and Sarah felt more alive than she had in weeks. The emptiness in her chest was still there but she was filled with a warmth that had been escaping her. They kissed her cheeks goodbye in turns after helping her clean up the kitchen. She felt the caffeine kick in and the coma she'd been living in seemed to be distancing itself for the moment.

Sarah took this stolen moment of warmth and energy and set about the cabin, tidying up the blankets and pillows, finally dragging her bags into her bedroom. She pulled back the heavy drapes letting in the sunlight. From the windows of the house, she was surrounded by glistening snow, like fields of shimmering glitter.

Letting the hot water run, steam filled up the bathroom while she unpacked her clothes into the dresser drawers. She selected a cozy sweater and jeans then set to brushing through her matted hair. She tried to remember the last shower she'd taken then cringed when she couldn't remember.

She stepped into the scalding stream of water and let

it pound against her tense shoulders. Working methodically, she shampooed and conditioned her hair, scrubbed her face, brushed her teeth, then scrubbed her body and shaved her legs. Not wanting to leave the comfort of the steamy bathroom, she wrapped her hair in a towel, tied on her terrycloth robe and tidied up her eyebrows in the mirror, stopping periodically to re-wipe a section of the fogged surface.

Taking time to put on lotion and blow-dry her hair, she felt a twinge of guilt at having plans. She imagined what it would be like if Daniel was here, if he hadn't died and they'd driven up to the cabin together. Daniel would have raced to the boathouse as soon as they pulled up. He would have insisted on taking the new kayaks out immediately, regardless of the ice, bad weather or wrong clothes. He would accept no excuses. They would have come in after a long paddle around the lake with frozen noses and fingers and Sarah would start a fire while he dragged in all their gear. They would make a nest in front of the fireplace of pillows and quilts and they would eat roasted marshmallows until they felt sick and passed out on the floor.

You always were the best marshmallow roaster, Sarah.

She jumped and spun around. Daniel's voice echoed in her ears, but no one was there. She shook herself and tried to reach out for a connection, but it was as always, a door slammed shut. It was good she was getting out of the cabin because she was obviously going stir crazy. A quick look at the clock at her bedside read 5:30 so she made quick work of dressing. She dusted off a bottle of wine from the cellar before wrapping on a scarf, pulling on some gloves, Daniel's jacket, a hat and heading out the door.

The dark of evening came early, but the clear sky kept the sparkle on the icy tree limbs. Although everything was a skeleton of its summer self, there was a beauty that was undeniable in the frosty stillness of the winter. She could smell a sweetness in the fresh crisp air that reminded her of maple syrup and pine. There was an odd satisfaction in the crunching sound of snow and ice under her boots as she made her way to the truck.

She hopped up behind the wheel, started the engine running, and climbed back out with the ice scraper from the glove box. Knocking snow from the windshield and scraping away the ice, the chill of the night began to bite into her cheeks and she could feel them turning red. Daniel used to say that her porcelain skin only had color when she was sun burnt or frost bit.

Get in the truck before you freeze to death. Daniel's voice reverberated in her skull and she stood frozen for a moment, ice scraper in hand.

"Daniel?" she asked out loud. No response came. *I'm going crazy…* she thought and she climbed into the truck. As she drove along the familiar road she thought about the familiar voice she'd heard twice now. Surely, her mind was playing tricks. It didn't feel like her imagination, though. She felt his voice in a deeper place, the place where she'd always been able to sense him when he was alive. Now when she tried to go there, to join him there, it was again an empty echoing chasm.

She pushed the thought away, turned off the main road and climbed the steep winding driveway up to Fred and Beth's cabin. Quaint and charming weren't enough to describe the cottage tucked away in the snowy clearing. During the spring and summer, a magical garden would emerge. Sarah had pretended she was Mary of The Secret Garden. Daniel insisted he was Colin and forced her to push him around the yard in a wheelbarrow. Once they met Jack, they made him play Dickon even though he had no clue what The Secret Garden was about or who Dickon was.

They invited Jack over to watch the movie version and when Dickon kissed Mary, Jack asked if he would have to kiss Sarah. "Of course not!" Daniel exclaimed with a little too much force. Jack assumed Daniel was being protective; Sarah knew otherwise. They didn't play Secret Garden again that summer.

Daniel told her what she'd already known when they were seven. He had just found out what "gay" meant and knew that this was who he was. Sarah didn't care, but she was afraid for him, and together they kept his secret.

Jack was Daniel's first crush. The summer the twins turned 12, Jack's family bought the old scout campgrounds on the other side of the lake. They got their first glimpse of Jack in the general store shopping with his parents. Sarah and Daniel were nearly always left up to their own devices and would ride their bikes up to Main Street where they would drink sodas from the rocking chairs of the general store porch. Beth would bring them slices of pie. Daniel and Sarah busied themselves, earning quarters from Fred by pulling weeds and stocking shelves.

One exceptionally warm summer morning, Sarah felt Daniel's heart skip a beat as she cut flowers for Beth. Turning to find him, she saw Jack approach and Daniel stock-still, staring. She blushed for him, and tugged at his shirt sleeve to break his trance.

"Don't stare!" she whispered.

"Just look at him..." he gasped and absorbing the blush from her cheeks onto his own, giggled in that guttural way that made it apparent his voice was on the verge of changing.

"Well, go talk to him then. Don't just stare. He'll think you're 'special'" she kidded and elbowed him in the ribs.

"Come with me?" Daniel pleaded.

The moments that Daniel found himself insecure were few and far between, but when they happened, it was almost relieving for Sarah. Daniel could make friends without a second's hesitation, but with every friend Daniel made, she felt further away and less needed by him. Any opportunity, like this one, to stand beside him as his strength and comfort, she seized with both hands.

Sarah pulled Daniel inside the market and they moved stealthily through the aisles scoping out their prey. They found Jack alone in the candy section. Sarah prodded Daniel forward, but his feet held fast. Reluctantly she stepped around him and approached Jack.

"What is your favorite?" she asked.

"Oh, um, I don't really have one." Jack said a bit startled.

"Daniel likes Sour Patch Kids," she jerked a thumb in Daniel's direction while he fumbled with a comic book, pretending he didn't see them, "I'm a chocolate person myself."

"I like Sour Patch Kids... Is that your brother?"

"Daniel, come here. Meet..."

"Jack, my name's Jack."

"I'm Sarah and this is Daniel." Daniel gave Jack a shy smile.

"Hi," Jack smiled. "So, you live around here?"

"Yeah, during the summers at least. We're the house on the far side. Your folks bought the old scout place right?" Daniel finally found his confidence and 'old charming' beamed out of his blue eyes.

"Sure did. We're fixing it up. Hoping to open in Spring. Lots to do, but my dad's pretty handy and he's teaching me. Says before I know it, I'll be building a cabin of my own."

"That's so cool; I'd love to know how to build things..."

Daniel was in his element and engrossed in conversation with Jack, so Sarah stepped back, pretending to be interested in a catalog for vegetable seeds then eventually walking back out of the store and returned to cutting flowers.

Sarah would have resented Jack if she didn't want Daniel to be happy so badly.

The summer memories faded and the winter filled back in around a shiny black king cab truck already parked next to Fred's Land Rover. "That must be Jack's," she thought aloud and a sudden shiver of nerves seized her stomach. Was she actually nervous to see him? Sarah tried to remember the last time she'd seen Jack. Could it really have been so long ago as their parents' funeral?

Don't be stupid, it's just Jack. His voice didn't startle her this time. She felt like Daniel was with her, anxious to see Jack himself. It didn't hurt her the way the memories did. It was as if he was actually there and she held onto that feeling, refusing to let it escape this time.

"Okay Daniel... let's go see Jack." She climbed out of the truck, tucking the bottle under her arm while shoving the keys into her coat pocket. Warmth radiated from the front windows and Fred met her at the front door. Sarah decided that she could never get enough of his hugs and he didn't rush releasing her either. Any chill she had from being outside faded.

"Now, you look like a bit of life has come back into those cheeks!" Beth bustled out of the kitchen, wiping her hands on her apron, pulled her into a hug then held Sarah's face for a moment, her warm hands bringing the feeling back to her frozen skin. She pulled Sarah in for another hug; this one like only a mother could give. Sarah breathed in the scent of jasmine perfume and apple pie. Tears suddenly stung her eyes.

"You thinking about Daniel, my girl?"

"Yes... and no. Always, really, but I... I'm just so sorry." Her ever-present stoic nature crumbled and her humanity flooded back in through the door Daniel cracked open when he connected with her just moments before.

"Sorry for what?"

"Sorry for not coming around more. Sorry for not calling you myself after Daniel."

"Now, now. That's not necessary."

"No, I mean it. You were always family to Daniel and me. It means so much to be here..." She blinked hard and Beth reached up to wipe away the overflow from her cheek.

"No apologies, my girl. You've been through the ringer and no one is gonna blame you for that. Now, you better get in this kitchen with me. I've got a pie just about ready to come out of the oven."

Sarah stayed back a second to wipe her eyes and take a few deep breaths before following Beth through the swinging kitchen door.

She stepped through the door with determination. Fred stopped mid-sentence to look up and give Sarah another big grin.

"Now, it's been too long since we've had this much young blood in our kitchen, Beth!"

"You've got that right, Pa." Beth pulled out the most tempting smelling apple pie and set it on the butcher-block island.

Sarah hesitated scanning the room to lay eyes on Jack. She had a new feeling in her stomach she'd never felt before.

There he is, she heard Daniel's voice in her ear. She realized that there were two sets of butterflies in her stomach, one hers, the other was felt on that slightly detached plane she'd learned to recognize as a child. She *was* feeling Daniel.

Before she could get too shaken up, Jack stood and closed the distance between them quickly. "Wow, Sarah. It's been so long." And before she knew it, she was wrapped in the warm comfortable embrace of a childhood friend she'd nearly forgotten. The butterflies faded slightly and as he released her, she made quick work of checking out the kid who'd grown up quite nicely since she'd last seen him.

Jack was taller than most, but not that skinny lanky tall. His hair was dusty blonde and his face had that "I haven't shaved in three days" scruff. His green eyes were piercing, but not hard. In his flannel shirt, faded jeans and worn hiking boots, he was just as she remembered him, but entirely different at the same time.

You've been in the city too long, sister. Daniel's voice again.

"I'm so sorry, Sarah."

She blushed a bit as she realized he still had her arms in his strong hands. The concern in his eyes made her want to comfort him. She could tell he really cared, just like Fred and Beth. She found herself hugging Jack again, this time by her initiation, his arms tight around her feeling right. The lake house wasn't such a bad idea after all... these people understood.

"No more sorrys," she smiled as she released him, "and that goes for all of you."

"You've got it, Chipmunk... no more sorrys. How do you feel about pork chops?"

"I feel very good about pork chops."

"Well, let's get this table ready and get some grub going!"

Beth made quick business of passing stacks of plates and silverware to Jack and Sarah who set the table while Fred carried over the steaming dishes of food. As Sarah sat and spread a napkin across her lap, her stomach growled and grumbled at every whiff of the delicious looking meal.

Holding hands around the table, Fred blessed the food, and Sarah felt at home.

"IT'S ALMOST TIME!" Fred called through to the kitchen from the living room.

Sarah backed through the swinging kitchen doors carrying the glasses of champagne she prepared and served them around. Fred and Jack began the countdown from their perches on the couch as Beth rushed to squeeze between them. Silently, Sarah slipped into the bathroom and gazed in the mirror at the closest thing she had to Daniel's face, "Happy New Year, brother."

Happy New Year, sister.

EIGHT

THE LAKE WAS freezing over faster than she anticipated. Immediately she regretted having not brought up the floating dock when they had left the lake house several months ago when the water was still bearable for swimming with the summer heat.

Daniel and Sarah had begged their father to build them this floating dock. Initially, he argued that the boat dock was plenty, but after a few stoking glares from their mother, he conceded to build the dock. It was quite funny since he didn't own tools and Fred, upon hearing the twins gush about the project, decided to "pop by" conveniently with a table saw and lent a hand.

When the deck was constructed and flipped upside down so that the buoys could be attached, Sarah got the great idea to fish out an old rusty bucket of paint from the crawl space.

They started by painting their names, then handprints, then foot prints until a full out paint war ensued.

Every summer it became tradition for Sarah and Daniel to race out to the floating dock (that Fred always just happened to put out for them before they arrived) and dive underneath. In the small air pocket formed by the buoys, they would try to remember whose handprint was whose, and they'd flip upside down to match their feet with the painted prints above. Each summer they would carve the year and their handprints in a row. After decades of carvings and handprints, there wasn't much area left on the underside of the dock.

Looking at the floating dock out on the still water, she knew she'd have to rescue the silly thing. She couldn't let the winter destroy this memory chest. So, reluctantly, she made her way through the un-shoveled path to the main dock and into the boathouse. The air seemed even colder in the dimly lit shed and she could see chunks of ice floating in the water through the boat launch opening. She found the end of the anchor rope and began pulling, but the slack in the line soon revealed a frayed end. The dock was floating free. Without a second thought she switched to plan B. She fought with gloved hands to release the closest kayak and let it drop hastily to the water below, shattering a thin icy layer that had already begun to form. Carefully lowering herself into the boat, the icy water splashed and stung the backs of her legs. She tucked a bundle of rope into the cavity of the boat and, getting a grip on the paddle, she inched her way out onto the lake, cracking the thin sheet of ice around her as she paddled.

The air bit into her face quickly and she almost decided to turn back. She could die if she fell in and with the bulky gloves she felt extremely awkward. As she reached the dock, she tied a rope to the top rung of the ladder, then the other end to the back of the kayak. Getting more frustrated trying to tighten the knots with her bulky gloves, she hastily jerked them off. Ice water splashed on her bare fingers as she double-checked the knots on the ladder all the while working to maintain her balance. She tugged to test the knots, but the thick rope kept slipping. Bracing herself with one leg in the kayak and one leg pushing off on the dock, she gave a fierce jerk to tighten the knots in a final effort.

Suddenly, she was surrounded by ice and darkness. Water rushed into her boots and Daniel's jacket dragging her under. In a fit for survival, she wrestled them off. Clawing at the expanse of water and ice between her and the surface, she managed to catch a gasp of air before sinking quickly again. She tried to open her eyes to search for the kayak or the dock floating somewhere above, but the stinging frost blurred her vision and all she could see was darkness. She kicked and clawed to the surface several more times, working her way towards the shore, but her limbs felt like they were encased in concrete, and soon she could only do her best to simply stay afloat.

As her legs cramped and her hands went numb, her body seized and she slid below the surface one final time. The thought of dying swept across her mind. Fear didn't come, but a sense of irony that this was the way she would go, devoured by the very lake she loved. She thought of Daniel, his last moments, and she hoped that he had the peace she felt as he realized the end was near.

Her arm seemed to catch on something and she found herself slightly irritated with the jerking pain. Then there was a body, a wrenching pull, then air. Through the numbness, she had a sense of being pulled into a boat and could feel the rhythmic movement that comes with violent rowing. She was hoisted into the air and carried then it got slightly warmer and she heard Daniel saying, *what were you thinking?*

SARAH STIRRED WITH a shiver although she was swathed in sweltering heat. Wet scalding towels were wrapped around her feet and hands and quilts cocooned her body. Jack was stoking the fire nearby wearing only a pair of Daniel's old pajama pants. She scoured her memories to try to discern what had happened. One moment she was paddling out to the dock then she'd been dying and Daniel had been there.

Jack noticed her waking and returned to the couch exuding a sense of calm although a riot of panic showed in his eyes.

"What happened?" she asked through chattering teeth.

"Well, it seems you decided it was perfect weather for a swim," he gave her a sideways grin.

"Funny."

"I pulled up to bring you something and when I couldn't find you in the cabin, I came down to the lake. Lucky I saw you really, you were already under."

"How'd you know?"

"I saw the kayak floating away and something just told me to jump."

"You swam from the dock? And you didn't even see where I was?"

"It was a strange feeling, like I could see you, or from your eyes, and it was so cold. I just knew."

"Huh."

"Yeah, huh is right."

He was sitting on the edge of the sofa and leaning slightly against her side. She could feel his heat through the inches of quilts between them.

"You scared the hell out of me."

"I'm sorry. Thank God you showed up. I already thought I was dead."

"Well, I'm glad you aren't dead, but we better get you checked out. Doc Paul's on his way."

"I'm okay. I swear." She struggled to get into more of a sitting position as chills continued to wrack her body. She saw a pile of wet clothes on the floor by the couch and suddenly blushed with the realization that those were hers and she was only wearing quilts.

Noticing the direction of her gaze, Jack cracked a hesitant smile. "I swear I didn't look."

She had the sudden urge to bury herself in the quilts and never resurface. He stood with the sound of the kettle whistle and filled several water bottles with the hot liquid. He let slip another sly smirk as she fussed with the blankets when he returned with the hot water bottles.

"Here you go. Let's get these on you."

"Thanks," she disrobed one arm to reach for the bottles. "Um, are you okay? Shouldn't you be bundled up yourself?" She was trying too hard not to look at his bare chest.

"You are probably right. Will you scoot?"

"Sure." Sarah curled to an Indian style position on the couch keeping the innermost quilt tightly around her and held a hot water bottle wrapped in both arms against her chest. Jack slid under a quilt, careful not to uncover her, and wrapped his arms around a hot water bottle of his own. They both sat Indian style, face to face, with icy toes touching under the blankets.

"So, what did you bring? More firewood?"

"No, although it looks like you may need more soon. Seriously, do you have a fire lit 24/7?"

"Guilty. Guess I'm a little too used to central heating."

"It was just some mail. Told Tom I'd save you the trip." He

reached around to the side table for a couple envelopes with the appearance of junk mail written all over them. His hand slid over hers and she felt herself begin to shiver again. They sat like that until a knocking at the front door jerked them away from the moment.

"That'll be, Paul." Jack hopped up from the couch to open the door.

"Hey Jack. See you've been working on warming her up." Sarah blushed behind frozen cheeks. "Hot water bottles were a good idea."

"I'll get some more water going in the kettle."

"Well, Sarah, decide to go for a swim, eh?"

This time she could only force half a smile and muttered, "Hi Doc," even though her jaw felt wired shut.

Paul, a tall gangly white haired man, was the last doctor on earth that Sarah knew made house calls. He hummed as he took her blood pressure and temperature then examined her hands and feet, checking for frostbite.

"Your temperature and blood pressure are still a bit low, but I think you're going to be all right. Jack, you'll stay with her tonight?"

"Uh, sure, yeah." Jack had found one of Daniel's hooded sweaters when he returned to them with reheated water bottles.

"Well, then, I'll get going, but you'd better call if she gets worse, all right?"

"Sure thing, Doc."

"I'm sure I'll be fine."

"I'll tell Fred you need some more wood. They'll probably want to come and check on you. You'd better get some rest, and call if you need anything, okay?"

"You bet."

Then he was gone and the house was, again, quiet with only Jack and the sound of crackling embers. He settled into the couch beside her and pulled her icy feet onto his lap and rested them on a hot water bottle, warming the tops with his bare hands. They remained there, motionless, until the hot water bottles dwindled to lukewarm against her skin. Her limbs, returning from their numbed state, began to ache.

"I wonder if a hot shower would help."

"Couldn't hurt. Let me help you up." He took care to keep a blanket covering her as he helped her stand.

Sarah moved slowly into the shower and, for a second time, drained the hot water tank. Warm and dry, she shuffled back into the living room in oversized cushy slippers to find that Jack had stoked the fire, straightened out the knotted quilts, made hot tea and boiled a can of chicken noodle soup.

"Get comfortable. You need to get this down."

Wrapping a knit afghan around her shoulders and covering her legs with a quilt, she drank down the soup and tea. The warm liquid reached the last few frosty places inside.

"Thanks for staying."

"No thanks needed." His smile warmed her more than the hot tea could.

A yarn bound notebook caught his eye from amongst a stack of books on the side table. He flicked on the lamp and, with a steaming cup of tea in one hand, flipped back the front cover.

"Is this one of yours?" he asked, angling the book so she could see the foreign familiarity of her own childhood scratchy scrawl.

"Looks like it."

"May I?"

"Be my guest." He read aloud, pages and pages filled with a child's serious attempt to sound like a literary prodigy, which resulted in giggles and smiles in the same child's 30-year-old counterpart. Sarah had to stretch to remember that little girl, but as the words came off each page, the sense of the child-hood writer seemed to seep into her soul and bit by bit, that young character became a familiar memory.

The editor inside kicked in and found several sections of the inexperienced manuscript to be pretty impressive for a 12-year-old. Something seemed to awake inside her as she remembered how much she had enjoyed writing. She wondered when that went away, when she stopped. She'd spent over a decade reading the writing of others and she couldn't remember the last time she wrote anything more than a to-do list.

I loved your stories, Sarah.

She whipped her head around looking for the source of the voice. It wasn't Jack; he was still reciting a poem about pine trees. She sat motionless reaching out with all her might to hear something more, but all that came were the sounds of the fire and snow falling outside.

At long last, fatigue took over and the sound of Jack's voice morphed into a rhythmic lullaby. It had been a long day: almost dying, sitting naked with a man that didn't assume any liberties, rediscovering a million childhood memories, and hearing the voice of someone who was not there.

NINE

SHE WOKE IN the morning to a knock on the door followed by the sound of two sets of boots knocking themselves clean as they stepped into the living room.

"Thank God, you're here. I was just going to get Paul. She's been tossing and turning since three AM and she's burning up." Jack's voice sounded stressed.

Trying to stand to greet her guests, the room began to spin, and she realized quickly that something felt very wrong. Beth was by her side in an instant.

"I just knew you would get sick! Poor dear, you're on fire. Let's get you tucked in." Sarah let Beth arrange the pillows and blankets into a thick cocoon. .

"I'll be back as soon as I can with the Doc." In moments Sarah heard Jack's truck roar to life and peal out long before the engine could have warmed up properly.

Beth draped her forehead with a cool rag and pulled off her socks. "We've got to get this fever down."

Sarah didn't put up a fight; she let Beth mother her, take her temperature, drank and ate what she was given even though fiery lumps had formed in her throat and each swallow burned and tore. Sarah could hear Fred stacking wood outside, and then she watched him out of the corner of her eye rebuilding the fire beside her. Chills began to shake her body and Beth methodically tucked the quilts around her and dabbed her forehead with a damp towel.

Reality became intangible as she drifted between wake and sleep. Daniel sitting silently on the floating dock, Fred stoking the fire, Daniel flipping through a photo album full of pictures of Jack, Beth resting her eyes in the wing-back chair pulled up close to the couch, Daniel staring back at her in the reflection of a mirror, Jack reading aloud the silly stories fed from her own pen.

All of a sudden she was sitting at the end of the dock; Daniel was stoking a bonfire out in the middle of the frozen lake. He turned, smiled, and beckoned her closer. Sarah slid down off the dock to the frozen lake below and inched out closer and closer to him. She called to him, but he did not speak, just smiled. The threads of cracking ice began to sound off under her feet and the fear of falling through again clung at her heart. He held out his hand to her as she neared. One more step and the floor shattered, their fingertips only a whisper away from touching, and she plummeted into the icy dark below. She tried to find the surface, but all was solid ice…

Beth stood hovering over her, telling her to drink, and ice cubes met her lips as a glass was tipped back. She'd never been so hot, so hot her very skin felt on fire. She moved to throw off the cover, but wasn't strong enough to lift them.

The scent of spring surrounded her as she climbed to her feet and out from under a mossy quilt in the center of a shaded glade. Sarah felt him close by, but couldn't see him. Suddenly his voice echoed out from the trees beyond.

A teenaged Daniel taunted, "You can't catch me!" She sped across the field and into the trees. The underbrush caught at her jeans and branches snagged her hair.

"Where are you!?" she yelled, tears filling her eyes.

"I'm here." A fully-grown Daniel appeared before her.

"Where have you been?" she scolded. "I've been reaching out to you and you disappeared."

"I'm dead, Sarah. I'm much farther away from you than I've ever been. The signal isn't as strong, if you will," a smile played at the corner of his mouth.

"It's not funny, Daniel! How could you leave me?"

"I wrote it all out in the letter. Do you really want me to dish out reasons? None of that matters now."

"I didn't read the letter."

"Why not? Didn't it stay with my body?"

"Yes, it stayed with your *body*! The question is why didn't *you* stay with your body? And I don't want to read about it! You're standing right here; I want *you* to tell me."

"Am I really standing here or are you just imagining me? You're fighting a pretty wicked fever right now, you could just be hallucinating."

"A fever? I feel fine."

"Look."

Suddenly they were standing on the front porch of the cabin, peaking through the window. Beth and Fred sat in chairs on either end of the couch and Sarah lay motionless under layered blankets with a red face and hair drenched in sweat. Beth reached out to feel the forehead of the sleeping Sarah. The porch faded and she could feel cool fingers against her brow and the fever raging in her body.

"Fred, will you pass me the thermometer? I think the fever's getting worse."

"If it's not any better when Jack gets back, we'd probably be smart to call the hospital."

"What can we do? The roads are impassable."

"I can't leave… I can't leave…" her voice was a rasp foreign to her.

"We'll see, don't you worry about that. Close your eyes and let me take your temperature."

Sarah obeyed. When she opened her eyes again it was sunset. She stood on the porch looking out at a fresh track of footprints in the snow leading out into the forest. She followed the tracks, her feet seamlessly finding each impression until she saw him sitting on a felled tree. A ring of melted earth encircled him and fresh grass and blooms were pushing their way skyward with time-lapse speed. Her first step into the circle brought back the scent of spring and dialed back the chilling bite of winter.

Sarah climbed up beside Daniel and reached for his hand as he automatically reached for hers. They sat like that, watching the plants around them form buds that arched into blooms, then fall back to the earth in endless loops. Caterpillars spun cocoons, and then burst forth in colors she'd never even imagined. Day turned to night, then back to day and she tracked the path of the sun and moon through the branches beyond. The trees themselves, first covered in snow and ice, then melting, left barren, then exploding with new growth and donning capes of moss only to bleed out orange and red into their leaves that floated away on the breeze leaving the branches barren yet again before the snow encapsulated them once more. Years could be passing, but she had no desire to move from that place.

"Why do you keep looking for me?"

"What else can I do? I was born to be by your side. I should be with you."

"No, we were created side-by-side, and we lived side-by-side, but it wasn't what either one of us was born for."

"Why are you saying this?"

"So you make the best choice."

"What choice?"

"Whether or not to wake up."

"I get to choose? I could stay here?"

"Yes, you get to choose."

"Then I choose to be with you."

"I can't guarantee that we would be together."

"What do you mean?"

"It's all more than I can explain."

"Well, then, what would you have me choose?"

"They want me to tell you to wake up."

"Who are they?"

"They don't want me talking to you. They tell me it's not your time. You won't live forever, you know. We'll get another chance," the smile was back at the corner of his mouth.

"When do I have to choose?"

"Now."

"But, will you still talk to me? Can't you reach out so I can feel you? You won't let them stop you, will you?"

"I'll always be there, whether you can tell or not."

"I can't… no," her tears opened up the skies and rain fell along as she cried.

Daniel held her face so close to his that she could see her reflection in his eyes, "Wake up, Sarah… Wake up!"

TEN

"WAKE UP, SARAH. Wake up."

Sarah's eyes snapped open to see Beth standing over her, mopping her forehead with a cold rag. "Your fever finally broke last night. You really had me scared there for a while."

A throbbing pulsed through her temples and her limbs ached as her mind rejoined with her body and the visit with Daniel faded farther and farther away. Her eyes began to well without her permission.

"Aw, dear, the worst is over," Beth wiped a lone tear from Sarah's check with the towel. "Think you can sit up? I made potato soup." Her smile was with bribery of Sarah's favorite meal.

"I'd like to try to sit at the table." Sarah's voice came out froggy and foreign.

"Are you sure?"

"Yeah. I need to move around."

Fred lent her a hand as she stood on wobbly legs and made her way to the dinner table. As she settled into the chair, the wood feeling cool against her back, the front door opened and in walked Jack.

"She lives!"

She worked her face into her best attempt of a grin.

He gave her a smile that left her feeling dramatically warmer. "You about ready, Fred?"

"Sure am." Fred pulled on his coat and headed towards the door.

"You take this with you, Jack." Beth pushed a large container of her famous soup into his arms.

"Thank you! Well, feel better Sarah. I'll stop in to check on you tomorrow."

"You're leaving?"

"Yeah, I just came to get Fred so we can get some work done at the shop and leave the car here with Beth."

"Oh, okay, I'll see you."

"It's a promise."

As they left, Sarah turned back to her soup, and she caught Beth giving her a strange smile. She turned back to the stove before Sarah could really analyze the look, but she returned to the table quickly with broiled garlic toast and without the odd look in her eyes. Sarah decided that any strangeness could easily be sopped up with Beth's garlic toast and she set in to devour the meal regardless of her aching head or scratchy throat.

"I'm glad you're feeling better; we were a little worried for a while there."

"I really am feeling all right. I'm sorry you had to deal with me like this. I was so stupid to fall into the lake in the first place."

"Don't be silly, Sarah. We didn't have to 'deal with you'. This is what you do for the ones you love, silly girl." She kissed the top of her head and filled her bowl a second time.

"Well, thank you."

"Anything for you, my dear."

Tears poured over her lids before she recognized the inescapable onset of sobs. She tried to breathe, but she was immediately in soundless, breathless, sobbing leaving her body racked in convulsions.

"Oh, my dear!" Beth's arms were around her in a moment and Sarah buried her face in Beth's blouse. She tried to breathe. She tried to stop, but it just wouldn't stop.

"Shush, shush, what's wrong?"

"I... I..." her wavering words barely escaped her mouth. "I thought I was dying... I saw Daniel. Then he was gone and I'm here and I don't know if I'm glad..." The sobbing took full hold and as she tried to speak again, all that could escape were elongated wailing cries.

"Oh, my girl," Beth rocked her ever so softly and, little by little, Sarah's breath caught up with her.

"I just miss him so much. Every time I think I'm going to be okay, I remember. I feel so guilty. I mean, how? How didn't I know? Why didn't I know? I should have known. I could have stopped him. I could have made it better." The sobbing threatened to swallow her again.

"Now, now. That's just not true." She rocked Sarah until her breathing became almost normal again. "Have I ever told you about Jennifer?"

"Jennifer?"

"Jennifer was our daughter."

"Was?"

"The summer before your parents bought this cabin— well, you two were just toddlers back then—I found out that Jennifer was sneaking out at night and rowing a canoe over to the scout camp to meet a boy. One night, she was out in the middle of the lake and, well, we don't know how it happened exactly, but she ended up in the water and…"

"She drowned? Oh God, Beth, I'm so sorry!"

"I'm sorry, sugar; I'm not telling you this to make you feel worse. It's just that, even today sometimes, when I think of what she would have been doing, what paths her life could have taken, I still feel like I could have done something differently. That I should have known, but the truth is I couldn't have. I don't understand why she had to leave us, but it happened. In the beginning I had to choose to be alive every moment of every day. It doesn't go away, but it does get better."

"And you stayed here? How could you bear to look at the lake every day after it took her?"

"You can't run away from the pain, Sarah. No matter how hard you try to tuck it away out of sight, it's not going to let go of you. I might as well see that lake every single day. It won't hurt any less to live somewhere else."

"I thought, if I came here, I'd feel better, you know. In a way I do, almost happy even, but… I'm afraid."

"Afraid of what?"

"That I'll lose those last few shreds of him I still had a hold on. Everything is just gone, likes he's been deleted from the world."

"You've just got to remember him, Sarah. Nothing can take away your memories."

They sat in silence for quite a while, Beth gently rocking and stroking her hair. Sarah let Beth's heartbeat regulate her own as the remaining tears turned into dry salty tracks on her face.

"Whatever happened to that writer that bought us out of legal pads every summer? You should write some of this out. They say journaling is helpful."

"Is that what *they* say?" She hated *them*. "Well, I've been trying to write since I got here and it's not going anywhere."

"Maybe that's why you can't write, you're working on the

wrong story." Beth kissed her forehead, and slowly loosened her embrace. "Now, if you are feeling strong enough, why don't you get yourself in the shower? I think four days is long enough. You'd better wash that hair."

"Ugh, four days? Really? Okay, I'm headed there now."

"I'll get your bed made up. I think it's about time you get off this couch."

"Aye, aye, captain."

She showered, pulled on one of Daniel's t-shirts, flannel pajama pants, fuzzy slipper socks and topped it all with an oversized "Columbia" hoodie over it all.

"How are you feeling?" Beth called from the living room. "Do you need pie?"

Yes, Sarah thought, *I definitely need pie.*

ELEVEN

CLARITY FOUND ITS way into her mind over the next few weeks and Sarah took to sitting at the desk with her laptop open, blinking cursor and blank page staring back at her. Most days, she broke up the sitting session with fresh coffee or staring at the snow covered trees, waiting in anticipation for the unavoidable giving way of branches dumping their frost loads to the ground below.

She would write a few sentences then swiftly delete them. She tried to write about the sky, the lake, New York City, Beth's potato soup... it all came out contrived. Taking a break, she dug out the child's manuscript and found a particularly funny written memory of Daniel climbing a tree. Reading it through several times, she tried to focus on what that day had looked like to those 12 year old eyes. The dirty Keds on her feet. The sting of scraped knees that had kept her feet on the ground while Daniel tried to scramble up the tree after Jack. Her stomach seizing with breathless laughter.

Sarah turned to the blank page and began typing at an unforgiving pace. Memories flooded the page. Days at the lake. Macy's Parades. The facts came out easily into words, but she couldn't quite find a way to explain the connection between Daniel and herself. Their secret language, the sense of each other that let them communicate without talking, the constant presence of the other that distance didn't seem to diminish. She couldn't explain these things on paper any more than she could explain how she kept hearing his voice.

A little light had been ignited inside her though, and something that felt so natural and energizing flowed through her veins as her fingers pounded away at the keyboard. Names and faces and places floated through her mind and as if the page and her mind were connected, they began to take form in the words before her. Hours and hours passed and she only took time to eat and sleep, but her mind powered on though her fingers stopped.

Keep going, Sarah. Bring me back. Daniel's voice faded in and out of her thoughts, twisted tendrils wrapping around those of her own, feeling a bit paler than the last few times she'd heard him. With each recovered memory of herself, the Daniel of recent days seemed to pale into a pastel sketch of himself in her mind. The 12-year-old boy was alive and well on the page and she held onto that. But the more she wrote about him, the more he lived on the page and not with her in the physical realm, where she could still feel him for fleeting moments at a time.

The apex of winter was marked by the complete freeze over of the lake. Through the window from her writing desk, Sarah watched snowmobiles skate across the icy surface, leaving behind an intricate basket weave of tracks.

A truck engine rumbled its way down from the main road to the side of the cabin and Sarah found herself hoping it was Jack. He had stopped by from time to time, bringing meals even though she insisted she was feeling fine. She had begun a mental tally of how much she owed him, Beth and Fred for all they had done for her since she'd arrived.

The particular sound of boots on the front porch confirmed it was Jack and he let himself in with the familiarity you can only find in small towns like Geneva. He kicked off his boots and dragged a kitchen chair over to where she was sitting. Turning it backwards, he sat resting his folded arms on the high back. His beard grew in more and more as the winter wore on but it suited him.

"How is the prodigal author this morning?"

"Hypnotized."

"A bit of writer's block, eh?"

"I wish you'd stop calling me an author."

"Not a chance." He gave her his mischievous smile. She returned it with her best grimace, but it only made him laugh. "Well, if you aren't on a roll, I propose a field trip."

"A trip? Where?"

"It's a surprise."

"You found a gold mine."

"Um, no."

"An elf colony?"

"You, dear, are ridiculous, but I won't take no for an answer, so get your boots on."

"So, you really aren't telling me?" Sarah reluctantly pulled on wool socks and her new snow boots and let Jack help her into Daniel's old coat. Sliding on the mustard yellow coat that she thought had been lost. "I still can't believe you fished this coat out of the lake."

"It was just floating there. Couldn't miss this color either. And nope, I'm not telling you. I'd make you wear a blindfold if I thought you would go along with it."

"Very mysterious," in her most sardonic tone.

Jack held the door for Sarah then closed it behind them. She headed for his truck, but was taken by surprise as Jack grabbed her hand. Startled by the feel of his hand on hers, she lost track of her thought. He released her hand as quickly as he'd grabbed it, though, and tucked his hands into his jacket pockets.

"This way," he said gesturing towards the lake with a slight nod of his head.

"We're going for a swim?"

"Nope, I've earned my Polar Bear Club membership for the year already." He let his elbow knock into hers as she joined him on the path toward the dock. As they reached the foot of the dock, he once again took an unexpected path and walked directly out onto the icy surface of the lake.

"Um… I'm not sure you got the memo. I barely got over the plague and I'm not exactly looking for ways to die today, so maybe we should stick to solid ground."

"Would I let anything happen to you?" His eyes met hers and she realized he meant this with all sincerity. He read the uncertainty on her face and reached out his hand. "Come on. Trust me."

"That grin, boy. It's evil," but she returned his smile and grabbed his hand. He let out a nearly silent chuckle. As she took the first step onto the ice, she felt him steady her.

He didn't let go of her hand this time and, for that, she was grateful. They walked quietly across the untouched snow leaving two sets of footprints as they went along. The sky was clear this morning and the bright sun lit up the ice below as if someone had sprinkled glitter over the whole lake. The bare trees along the edges glimmered like chandeliers with the ice and snow coating their branches. Looking up toward the mountainside, the gray and brown netting of dormant trees were broken up by the deepest green pines dusted perfectly with a powdery dose of flakes. She'd forgotten how sweet the winter could be.

"Almost there." She hadn't noticed where they were going or how close they were to the opposite shore, but snapping out of her reverie, she saw that they were nearing the old campsite.

"You're taking me camping?"

"Stop trying to guess!" He laughed heartily this time and she couldn't help but smile. There was something about him that was purely infectious. He squeezed her hand and smiled at her, a smile that made her hold her breath.

They reached the shore and he helped her off the ice. Hand in hand, they trudged through the deep snow up towards a semicircle of cabins, their freshly painted facades basking in the warm glow of the fading sun as it set over the water.

"You wait here." He knocked the snow off one of the wooden benches arranged in a ring around the bonfire pit then darted off towards the largest of the cabins. She sat, feeling an instant chill take the place of his hand. The snow had been shoveled away from the center of the pit and dry wood was arranged for a fire. The camp had fallen into disrepair after Jack's father abandoned his project after a decade. As she looked around, though, she was surprised that the place looked like it had never felt the effects of weather or time.

"You remember this place?" Sarah jumped at Jack's voice which, naturally, made him laugh once again.

"Of course," she said, trying to regain her composure yet

feeling the burn of blush on her cheeks. "You did all this?"

"Yeah, still one more cabin to do on the inside, then the rest has to wait till the thaw." He'd returned with a large basket and a blanket that he wrapped around Sarah's shoulders. "No pneumonia relapses for you." He knelt beside the wood pyre and made quick work of starting a blazing fire. She watched him spread out a second blanket nearer to the fire where the snow had been shoveled away revealing the flagstone below and begin to arrange the contents of the basket in front of him. "You'd better get over here."

Tightening her hold of the thick wool blanket around her shoulders, she stepped over to the newly assembled picnic, knocking the snow from her boots before she sat.

"I can't remember the last time someone fixed me a picnic."

"I can. It was you."

"What? I fixed a picnic?"

"Yeah, well, I'd call it a picnic. You made PB&Js and carted a whole six-pack of root beer to the top of Mulligan Pass."

"I don't know if that counts. To be a picnic there must be a basket and a blanket. Now *this* is a picnic." She gestured to the impressive spread he was laying before her.

"Nah, you've got your facts a bit off. I looked it up and everything."

"Oh, well, don't let me question Wikipedia." She smiled a real smile as he laughed. The sound of it was warmer than the fire growing steadily at his hands.

"Never question the Wiki," he returned her smile and settled beside her, his knee grazing hers as he folded his legs Indian-style. "So what'll it be? Hot dog? Or you wanna live on the edge and start with dessert?"

"Dessert for sure."

"You're such a heathen!" He pretended to look shocked. "S'mores it is!" He stuck marshmallows on shish kebab skewers and passed her one, "and I brought extra chocolate for the chocolate person."

"How do you remember so much? That was so long ago."

"Aw, not *so* long. I mean, it's been…" he looked off to the tree tops doing silent math in his head.

"It's been 12 years since I saw you last."

"No! Really?"

"It's true."

"Well, never mind that. I'm betting you still remember my favorite candy too."

"Sourpatch Kids."

"See, we aren't old and senile just yet. So that means we've known each other for 18 years… that's most of our lives."

"So what else do you remember?"

"I remember counting down the days every year until we'd be back at the lake. I couldn't wait to see you and Daniel. I still have stacks of letters from Daniel, but you, you didn't write letters." He stared into the fire for several long moments, with a look she couldn't decide if it was regret or sadness. "Now, your turn."

"Hmmm," she thought while assembling a s'more with two blackened marshmallows. "I remember…" she squinted trying to pick a memory out of the fog that was her mind.

"Oh come on."

"Okay, I remember when Daniel kissed you."

"Ha! Ha! Yeah, he sure did! I was so surprised! He'd looked at me so seriously and held my shoulders. He said, 'Now just hold still. I have to do this.'" Jack demonstrated by grabbing Sarah by the shoulders and staring her in the eyes. "Then, holy hell! He planted one right on me!" He released her, letting his hands slide down her arms before letting go completely. "That was my first kiss you know." Jack's laughter spread to Sarah and soon they were both clutching their sides and gasping for air through their hysterics.

"And you! You told Daniel all serious like, 'I'm sorry, Danny, but I don't think I like kissing boys.' Then Daniel…" she dissolved again into a breathless laugh.

"Then Daniel says, 'Well you'd better try kissing a girl to see if you like it any better' and I said 'but I don't know any girls!'"

"That's when I punched you and shouted, 'I'm a girl, you idiot!'"

"Then I kissed you." He'd stopped laughing and gazed at her with that distant glint of sadness again.

"That was my first kiss… with a boy trying to check and see if he liked girls."

"No, I knew I liked girls. I knew I liked you."

"What!?" Her laughter turned nervous, and she forced her eyes to find another place to rest.

"Hey, I saw an opportunity, had to take it," his smile was so wide it seemed it would crack.

"Well, here's to seizing opportunities," she announced then smashed a gooey marshmallow over Jack's nose.

"No!!!!" His laughter spread to her as he tackled her smearing one of his marshmallows across her cheek. Just as suddenly they both became aware of the closeness and grew silent. The tension hummed in the air intertwined with the cracking of the fire. Jack spoke first, "I knew a girl like you wouldn't ever like a boy like me."

"I guess you'll never know."

Jack returned to his cross-legged position. "Guess not."

"So," trying to shake off the electricity still moving through her limbs and cleaning the marshmallow from her face, "what kind of girl was I exactly?"

"Oh, you know. Smart, kind, good at everything… beautiful."

"What kind of boy were you that a girl like me wouldn't like you?"

"Oh, I don't know."

"Well, I thought you were great. Smart, kind, *and* beautiful.

Not good at everything but, hey, we can't all be that good." She nudged him with her knee through the wool blanket.

"That last year I don't think you thought I was that great. You looked at me like I was ruining your world. Dad said not to take it personal, that you were being ruled by hormones."

"I'm sure hormones weren't helping, but, I guess I was jealous."

"Jealous? Of what?"

"It's just, well, Daniel wanted to be around you more than me. I was the third wheel and that had never happened before with us."

"You didn't have separate friends?"

"Not really. We were always the most important person to each other. I mean, it's hard to explain…"

"Try."

"We could hear each other in a way. We always knew what the other was feeling and sometimes it was like having a conversation with each other."

"Isn't that an identical twin thing?"

"I know they say that it shouldn't really happen with fraternal twins, but it was always there with us. Even when we were babies. Mom told us she'd been so worried that we would never speak. We had our own made up language, but didn't have a need for 'real' words."

"If your bond was so strong, why would you think that we were edging you out?"

"Daniel had never blocked me out, but with you, he wanted to hold some things back from me. It was the first time he really wanted something outside of 'us'."

"I never realized…"

"Hey, it was still the best time of my life, so we don't need to get all serious." She smiled and tried to bring back the levity to the conversation.

"Likewise. Even getting kissed by a guy wasn't so bad. I mean, Daniel was one hot 16-year-old."

"He really loved you, you know. He cried for days when you told him that your family wouldn't be coming back the following summer."

"Hell, I cried! But it was probably for the best. It let Daniel get over me… gave me time to get over you."

"Get over me?"

"Oh, come on. I had it so bad for you! Don't pretend like you didn't know."

"No, you didn't."

"Yes! Daniel never told you?"

"I guess Daniel was better at secrets than I was."

"Hey, sorry. I didn't mean to bring up."

"No," she touched his knee, "it's okay. Even if I knew, we couldn't have been anything more anyways."

"See, we're back to you being too good for a guy like me."

"No! It's just, you were Daniel's whether you felt the same way or not. I couldn't do that to him."

"So… am I still Daniel's?" He gave her a sly sideways grin.

"That's yet to be determined." She poked around in the fire with the shish kebab skewer. He didn't realize the seriousness with which she'd been asking the same question. "So, what happened anyway? Why did your family leave?"

"Ah, mom got word that her cancer was back so we had to head back to town so she'd be closer to the hospital."

"Oh my gosh, Jack! You never told us that. We could have… I don't know, but we would've come to see you."

"I didn't really understand what was happening then. It was all sorts of going through the motions. I just remember being mad that my world had been turned around. Then she took a turn for the worse out of nowhere. She died that November."

"I'm so sorry…"

"It was hard, harder on Dad, I'm sure. He was never really the same."

"Was? Where is he now?"

"Let's just say, he decided to follow her a few years ago." He hung his head and fiddled with loading a hot dog on a skewer and blinked in fast flutters.

"Jack…"

"It's hard all over, isn't it? I mean, I remember being at your parents' funeral and thinking, 'Buck up, Jack. At least you still have one parent. Imagine losing them both on the same day.' But when Dad was gone, I realized I had lost them the same day… his ghost just lingered a while longer."

"I wish we had known. I mean, you were alone. It was hard on us, but we had each other. We would have been there for you."

"I know," he squeezed her hand and wove his fingers with hers. "I don't think I wanted anyone then, though. I just worked more. Then just this past April, I was sitting at my desk, writing the check for the property taxes for this place and the light bulb went off. I'd been working as an architect in San Francisco for years and bored by every day of it. I quit my job that day, packed my apartment into the bed of my truck and drove across the country to get here. At first I thought I'd just spend a few months fixing the place up, then sell it, buy a boat, and never set foot on land again, but reconnecting with Beth and Fred and everyone else in this town… this place just has something. Something good, you know? The time I spent here has always been the best in my life, and I want to give more kids that chance. I started talking to the pastor of the church my mom went to in the city and we are creating a foundation that raises money to send groups of inner city kids up here a week at a time starting spring break and running all summer. If everything lines up, I'll have my first set of campers in a couple months."

"That's amazing! Well, if you need an extra set of hands around here, I'm not exactly busy."

"Oh yeah? How are you with a paint brush?"

"Well, according to you I'm good at everything, remember?"

"You're definitely good at more than you know." She gave him a quizzical stare, but he only returned it with a slightly burnt hot dog in a bun. "Eat up."

TWELVE

EVERY BIT OF movement seemed louder against the backdrop of utter silence as she drove toward town. She tried to think of a word for the way the thick layer of snow seemed to shimmer back at her. *Radiant? Not exactly.* It was breathtaking nonetheless. She recognized the hollow churning feeling as hunger. So strange that her mind needed time to remap around the dead Daniel places in her brain so it could slowly resume normal function.

As she neared town, her phone rang. "Hello?"

"Sarah! Sarah, it's Celeste."

"Hey, I've been meaning to call."

"Well, you've had us all worried. Marie Claire told me about your accident. I was surprised to hear you asked her to send you more work."

"Yeah, I think I'm going stay up here for a while longer.

I'm not ready to come back just yet."

"No, I understand completely. It's just that Marie Claire came running into my office this morning in a panic over your email. She thinks you must have hit your head or something. She went on and on about it being a cry for help."

"What? Now I'm confused."

"She said you asked specifically for a cookbook to edit."

Sarah couldn't help but laugh, "Yeah, but I wasn't aware that would warrant a call to the authorities. I was thinking that something different would be good, and heck, I never did learn to cook so I might as well test some recipes while I work."

"All right, well, I'm glad you haven't lost your mind up in that wilderness. We'll get some things together for you. The city will still be here when you decide to come back, so don't rush."

"Thanks, Celeste."

Main Street spread before her and she pulled up next to Jack's truck at the hardware store. Sarah couldn't put a finger on the moment she decided to let him in, but he was indelibly present in her mind and it made her glad. The familiar jingling of the bells sounded as she pulled open the front door and the smell of pine surrounded her with warm air.

"Chipmunk, is that you?" Fred called from the back of the store.

"Yeah, it's me." She meandered through the aisles until

she found him.

"Jack just ran a load of wood down to Tom's place for me. He shouldn't take very long, but Beth's up at the house if you want to go say hi."

"Sure, I'll head up there now."

Sarah let herself out through the back of the store that turned immediately into a narrow path arched over with intertwined branches. The morning sun hit each tiny icicle to line the walk with diamonds. She stretched her gait to step in the boot prints left from Fred's walk to make the uphill trek in deep snow more manageable. The path emerged from the trees into the cozy clearing and led right up to the back stairs of the cabin. The door swung open as Sarah kicked a lower step to knock the snow from her boots.

"Just in time! I could use a hand with these pies!"

Sarah smiled. It never got past her, the strangeness of finding such down home Southern cooking in the middle of Vermont. You couldn't go much more North without turning Canadian. Fred and Beth moved North on a whim brought on by a showing of *White Christmas* and they'd had their fair shares of white Christmases as a result, but their accents never faded and the amount of butter in Beth's pie crusts, thankfully, had never changed.

Beth set Sarah to work cracking pecans as she rolled out pristine circles of dough on the floured butcher's block. Time passed quickly with Sarah's repetitive motion of cracking each shell in the exact perfect place to reveal unbroken pecans.

"So, you've been seeing a lot of Jack these last weeks."

"Uh, yeah. He's been sweet, checking on me. He's still taking care of Daniel's sister after all these years."

"Do you really think he's only coming around out of loyalty to Daniel? I'm pretty sure he doesn't just see you as Daniel's sister… not anymore."

Before Sarah had to respond, the phone rang.

"Oh, hi dear. I'll let her know." Beth set the phone back in the cradle. "Perfect timing! I tell ya! That was Fred. Jack's just got back to the shop." She caught the timer at the beginning of the buzz and pulled out a piping hot pie from the oven. "You're taking this with you."

The walk downhill was a little more treacherous as she battled both the incline and the scalding heat of the pie even through its cardboard box and her thick leather gloves. Watching her step more than the way in front of her, she nearly impaled Jack with pecan pie. Jack caught her arms at the elbows as she regained her footing. *Nice one* reverbed the familiar tone in her skull.

Sarah met his eyes and his ever-present smile and the frost biting at her legs melted away.

"You sure you're ready to get dirty?"

"I'm ready if you are."

"Hope you don't mind, I threw some paint cans in your truck."

"'Course not."

"You remember the way?"

"I'll follow you."

Sarah's truck followed Jack's as he turned left off of Main Street onto Lake Drive instead of making her usual right turn, the cab filled with the aroma of fresh baked pie. Most of the houses along the lake were on the south shore, like Sarah's, because the land of the camp encompassed the majority of the north shore. A few minutes later, she was torn from staring at the back of Jack's head, when he made the turn into the entrance. She could barely make out the camp sign and caps of all the new post and rail fencing poking through the tops of the snowdrifts.

She parked beside Jack's truck in front of the main cabin. He grabbed two gallons of paint from the bed of her truck and followed him inside, thankful for the warmth of the pie in her hands.

"Welcome to mi casa."

"Nice place you got here. You've already done a lot."

"Here," he took the pie from her, set it on a side table, and grabbed her hand, "let me show you around." She let him lead her through the main living space, the small kitchen and through the two bedrooms. All the while, she listened to him talk about refinishing floorboards and retrofitting windows, but all she could focus on was the feel of his hand around hers.

"So, I figured we'd start in here."

"Start what?" Sarah's eyes darted nervously around the bedroom.

He lifted the hand he'd been holding and replaced his palm with the handle of a paint roller. "Painting, of course."

She hid her blushing by wrangling the first paint can open and getting straight to work. They painted to his playlist of Louis Armstrong, Duke Ellington and Ella Fitzgerald, coating each room in newness until all that was left was the wide foyer they'd entered through hours before.

"Let's take a break, I'm starving." His voice cut through the last line of *How High the Moon*, startling her out of her fume-induced daze. "I'll whip up some grub." Sarah followed Jack into the kitchen and leaned against the island while he assembled sandwiches and hot soup onto a tray. "There's a couple blankets in the bench by the door."

All the furniture in each room was piled and covered in plastic so they returned to the entryway where light streamed in through the floor to ceiling windows that flanked the front door. Sarah spread out one of the blankets she'd retrieved from the bench and they settled down on the floor.

"We're really making this picnic thing a habit, huh?"

"I told you," Jack passed her a steaming bowl, "I'm a sucker for a picnic... that and I'm short on chairs at the moment. Sorry, there's no heat up here." Jack tossed a second blanket over both of them, taking the time to tuck the edges tightly around her legs.

He hesitated slightly, "Do you remember my first summer here? You and Daniel let me help with your time capsule and we closed it up in the wall of one of the cabins?"

"Of course I remember." In fact, she'd buried that memory away a long time ago, but it resurfaced like a rare treasure.

"Well, after I heard about Daniel, all I wanted to do was tear into the wall to get it back. I just wanted to find something close to him after he was gone. I even went over to your cabin and sat on the porch on Christmas Day just rereading his letters and replaying memories. I couldn't imagine him not being here. I still can't." He paused, searching her face for a reaction. After a few silent moments, he asked, "Are you upset?"

"Where is it?" she asked quietly, feeling a sense of panic tinged with excitement well up in her stomach.

He bounded up and placed a hand on the wall, precisely as if trying to feel a heartbeat. "Right behind here."

"Hmmm."

"Hmmm? What do you think? If you want me to rip through the wall this is really the best time. I'll be less inclined once I've painted and put up new baseboards."

Her mind churned. She wanted to see it, but it also felt like exhuming a body.

"I mean, time capsules ARE supposed to be opened again someday, right?" He watched her as she stared at the spot like she was working out a complex math equation.

"Let's do it."

"Get up!" A boyish grin stretched across his face as he dug through his toolbox then handed her a hammer. "It's gotta be you. Just give it a good swing right here."

"I dunno… maybe you should."

"Nope, this is all you. Call it a step in the grief process."

She stood staring at the spot where Jack had pointed. Her heart pounded and she had the sudden urge to run.

"It's okay, Sarah." Jack set an encouraging hand on her shoulder and his warmth spread down her back and slowed her heart to a normal pace. "Take your time."

She took a deep breath in, allowed the seam into her sealed up pain to part just the slightest bit, and slammed the hammer into the wall all the way up to the handle.

"Whoa!" Jack exploded into laughter. "Are you okay? Did you smash your hands?" Sarah released the hammer and let her hands fall into Jack's for examination. There were tears in her eyes, but she blinked them back. "They look okay, does it hurt anywhere?"

"My hands are fine."

"Better let me finish this off," he smiled at her as he wiggled the hammer free from its drywall captor. Sarah returned to the warmth of the blanket on the floor and watched Jack as he worked.

He inserted a small saw into the hole she'd made and cut a neat square, letting the freed pieces of the plaster board fall to the floor. He reached his arm up to his elbow inside the cavity behind the drywall then slowly, as if retrieving the most fragile of eggs from a birds nest, pulled out a newspaper wrapped package, never allowing it to bang against the edges of the opening.

After eighteen years in a wall, the newspaper disintegrated as Jack unfolded the protective sheets to reveal a rusty metal lunch box with the familiar face of He-Man on the lid. As he carried the box back to Sarah, Jack held it up like a reverent sacrifice. Sliding back under the blankets and facing her again, Sarah was surprised by a jolt in her gut as his crossed legs met hers when he scooted closer and placed the box between their laps.

"We don't have to open it right now," reading her uncertainty.

"No, it's all right." Their eyes locked, and she saw someone who truly loved Daniel, missed him, like she did. Again the giddy tingle that was so foreign yet seemed natural shook through her appendages. She tore her gaze from his green eyes to the cover of the box. "Let's open it."

Jack helped shimmy the rusted metal latch open and left the unveiling to Sarah. As she lifted the lid on its hinges and let it fall back against Jack's thigh, the memories of laughter and sunlight and the chilly mountain lake poured out. Jack leaned forward and she could feel him watching for her reaction and letting her take her time to rummage through the contents.

Three matching friendship bracelets, an empty "gum tape" container, one beaded earring (its match residing somewhere at the bottom of the lake), a tattered origami fortune teller, a bottle of "Clear Coke" and at the bottom, a ribbon-tied roll of paper and a faded photograph of three gangly 12-year-olds with watermelon smiles encased in a hot-glued popsicle stick frame. She took each item out ceremoniously, examined, smelled, and then passed into Jack's waiting hand. He regarded each item with a wistful smile then set each one gently inside the lid in a tidy arrangement. The removal of the scroll left the container empty. She played with the still perfect bow.

"Shall we?"

"Here," she placed the paper in his hand. "You do the honors."

Jack gently slid the ribbon, releasing the tight coil and unscrolled the page just enough to read the contents aloud.

> *To whichever soul shall discover this treasure,*
>
> *We are writing to you from the year 1992. We are 12 right now, but are most likely dead and gone (or old and gray) as you read this. You should know that if you've found this because you are tearing down the camp for skyscrapers, you will suffer the curse of the ancient Indians that once lived on this land. If you respect the magic of the lake, you'll never again feel pain and will live forever (well, most likely).*

*If your intentions are pure, add your treasures to
ours in this time capsule, and bury it again beneath the
tallest tree on Mulligan Pass. You'll know the right one
because it has our initials carved there and we made a
circle of rocks around the base.*

S.D.J.

"Well, we were a bit dramatic back then," Jack's smile
turned sad. "Daniel made you add the part about the Indian's
curse." Sarah fiddled with the ribbon and stared out at the
slowly fading afternoon sun.

"What are you thinking?"

"Honestly, I don't know what to think, but it makes me
feel…" She wasn't sure what it made her feel and Jack didn't
push for an answer. Jack took another turn lifting each item in
his hands then placing them back into the container with rev-
erence. When everything was resting again inside the lunch-
box, he closed the lid and set it beside him on the blanket.

"You know, Daniel's gone. You're allowed to be sad. It
might feel better right now to bottle it all up, and that's fine,
but if you never let it out, it'll eat you alive."

"Yeah. It's just, if I feel it all, I think I'll just dissolve or
something. I tried the whole 'working through it' thing with
a therapist a few years after my parents died, but I just became
a drone. We were so close. I guess it's easier to just live like
he never left."

"That won't make you happy forever."

"And that's why I'm trying to stay busy. That seems to help. I'm having more work sent. At least, until I'm ready to go back to the city."

"It's funny. You never struck me as one who would love living in the city."

"I don't hate it. I mean, it's where my family was rooted. We lived in that apartment our whole life."

"Daniel moved, though, didn't he?"

"Yeah, but it was just because of the noise he made when he was sculpting. He always came back to me. And, I mean, it's where I work. It just makes sense, I guess."

"And your work, you like what you do, right?"

"Sure, I mean, I'm good at it. I like who I work with." She wasn't sure where this conversation was going.

His hands slid into hers and her eyes were drawn away from the floorboards and up into his eyes as if by an unseen force. "If I've learned anything at all, it's that you've got to do something that makes you happy, not just something that keeps you busy. I mean, this could be an opportunity to really think about what *you* want."

"I can't think too much and right now, thinking isn't good. It hurts too much."

"Life on autopilot isn't exactly a life."

"Well, it's working right now. Did you prefer coma girl? Because that's all that's left of me when I acknowledge Daniel is dead and my whole life is over."

The silence carried the heaviness of the world. Sarah couldn't bring herself to look into his face.

"You done eating? I'll clean up." Jack got to his feet, not waiting for her response before picking up her bowl and plate.

Sarah folded the blankets, tucked them away in the bench then stood in the entry in a struggle between fight or flight. Every molecule of her wanted to run out the door and drive away, but his presence in the other room kept her anchored to the floor.

Jack returned with the pecan pie and two forks. "A peace offering?"

"Peace it is," she smiled and reached for a fork. "I'm sorry."

"No apologies, just pie."

THIRTEEN

SARAH WAS AN hour into dinner prep mode when she decided that coq au vin had been a huge stretch for her non-existent culinary skills. She didn't care how big of a TV star the smiley, big headed, French girl on the cover happened to be. If this meal wasn't a hit, her book would never see the printing press.

As if on cue, Jack walked in just as she finished braising the leeks and was making sure the chicken was finished.

"Mmmmm... smells amazing," he hummed as he pulled her into a hug despite her oven mitted hands. His grip around her ribs triggered a laugh and she was almost certain he'd lingered to smell her hair. "I brought wine." He released her to display the two bottles he held in one hand by their necks.

"Nice, let's crack one open."

Jack dug the wine key from a cluttered drawer and opened

a bottle, pulling four wine glasses from one of the kitchen shelves. For just a moment, she had forgotten that Fred and Beth would be there soon and suppressed a desire for a quiet night alone with Jack.

"Want me to set the table?"

"That would be fantastic. Sorry, this sauce is taking longer to reduce than this silly book says it should."

"No prob. Table cloth?"

"In the armoire in my room. There are napkins in there, too."

She returned to stirring her pot, kept company by the butterflies in her stomach, while Jack spread out the tablecloth and pulled dishes and silverware down to set the table.

"Do you have music?" he asked.

"Uh, just Pandora."

"That'll do. Do you mind?" He sat down in front of her laptop.

"No, no at all. Here, let me put in my password." She leaned around him to type in the extensive string of characters. Suddenly, Daniel was smiling back at them both.

"Daniel," was all he could say as he sat back hard in the chair as if he'd been shoved in the chest.

"Sorry," she quickly launched a browser window to hide his face.

"No," he reached and covered her hand holding the mouse, directing her movement and pressing her index finder to minimize the browser window. "I haven't seen his face in so long. When was this taken?"

"Two summers ago," she leaned against the armrest with her spare hand, the other still held captive between Jack and the mouse. "We'd spent the whole day out on the lake."

"He looks so happy."

"I thought he was."

"I'm sure he was."

"I'm not sure about anything anymore. I mean, you don't leave the way he did if you were happy."

The sound of tires crunching through snow disrupted the conversation and Jack released her hand. Subtle notes of jazz began to play behind her as she returned to the stove, refusing to turn away until she regained her composure and the sauce was perfect.

"Hey, you made it!" Jack's voice had returned to its typical jovial tone as he opened the door for Fred and Beth.

"Sorry we're a bit late. I was waiting on this pie." Beth held up a tin foil wrapped dish in her worn pink mittens. Pie seemed to be Beth's love language.

"Not at all," Sarah turned with her best painted smile, "perfect timing."

She took turns with Jack hugging both Fred and Beth then surveyed the table. Jack had set the table with precision and decorated the center with candles she didn't remember owning.

"Look at this!" Beth gasped, as she set her pie on the counter next to the tray of braised leeks and potatoes and the covered dish containing the chicken.

"Who knew Chipmunk was a chef!" Fred slid his coat off into Jack's waiting hands.

"Well, that remains to be seen. You haven't tasted it yet."

"How can I help, dear?" Beth slipped off her jacket and returned to the kitchen.

"Help me bring these to the table?"

"What can I do?" asked Fred.

"You take a seat and get prepared to lie to me if it tastes terrible."

Fred settled in, Jack filled up the wine glasses and Sarah and Beth carried the food to the table. Sarah tugged at the knotted ties of her apron, but was getting no results.

"I'm totally making this worse," she frowned.

"Here, let me help you." Jack was behind her, fussing with the knots before she could protest. Fred and Beth exchanged knowing looks that made Sarah blush and avert her eyes. "Got it!" He slid the apron off over her head and held out the chair for her.

"Thanks," she was sure she was blushing wildly now as she let him slide the chair under her as she sat. "Will you do the honors, Fred?"

"Of course," he said, holding out his hands in expectation. The four joined hands around the table as Fred blessed the food, although the tingling in the hand Jack held distracted Sarah from hearing the words.

"OH BOY," FRED moaned, sliding back his chair and rubbing his stomach.

"Is that a food-was-good 'oh boy' or a massive-indigestion 'oh boy'?" She'd thought the meal had been okay, but was a little concerned with how quiet everyone had been as they ate.

"It was an I'm-not-sure-I've-got-room-for-pie 'oh boy'."

"Now, don't you say that! Can't let this pie go to waste!" Beth stood and began clearing plates, waving off Sarah's protests to leave them.

"Let me help," Jack leapt from his seat and started scraping plates.

"Really now, who wants pie?" Beth pulled down a stack of clean dishes. A round of "me"s sounded and Sarah leaned back in her chair, letting Beth and Jack serve up dessert.

"You did an excellent job, Chipmunk." Fred smiled at her in a food-induced haze.

"Well, thanks. I'm glad it turned out."

"Maybe you'll be up to cooking something special for Jack's birthday," Beth suggested. "I'm afraid my only real specialty is pie."

"You didn't tell me your birthday was coming up. When is it?" Sarah asked Jack.

"Next week. But, like I told them, I'm not big on birthdays."

"It's decided. We'll break in your new kitchen," Sarah announced determinedly.

"Oh good!" Beth clapped as she rejoined the table. "You just tell me which pie to bring, Jack."

Sarah took a bite of pie, and feeling his gaze on her, turned to meet his eyes. Jack gazed at her with a smile she hadn't seen before and he didn't look away. Finally, it was Sarah that broke the locked trance. She gave quick glances toward Fred and Beth, but it seemed they were too invested in their pie to notice the staring contest. Jack's knee pressed against hers under the table and she returned to the pull of his gaze. Together, they finished their slices as well.

After the coffee had gone cold between all the small talk, Beth and Fred announced it was getting too late for them.

"Thanks so much for coming, guys," Sarah embraced Beth with all the warmth she had in her.

"It was our pleasure, dear."

"Thanks for having us, Chipmunk," Fred gave her hand a squeeze. "You coming, Jack?"

"Uh…" he was loitering in the kitchen still, "I think I'm gonna stay and help clean up."

"Right," Fred gave Jack a wink that wasn't meant for Sarah's eyes, but she caught it regardless. "Goodnight."

"G'night, drive safe." Sarah watched from the porch as

they got into their truck and pulled out of the driveway. Stepping back inside and closing the door behind her, the wall of heat stung her bare hands and the sight of Jack, stoking the fire, lit a flame in what had been an empty place in her heart that she couldn't quite comprehend.

She pried away her fixed eyes and busied herself with loading the last of the dishes into the dishwasher and setting the cooking pans to soak.

"Leave those."

She jumped at the sudden closeness of his voice and spun to find him right behind her. "You scared me!"

"Sorry." He traced her arm from her elbow to her hand with two fingers, "dance with me?"

"To this? You can't dance to jazz."

"I would dance with you to silence."

She surrendered with a small step towards him and a raised hand to meet his shoulder. One hand took hold around her waist while the other enfolded her hand. She could feel his heart beat against hers, beating in entirely different melodies to each other and the music.

Slowly they swayed with no aim at rhythm or concept of time. She rested her head against his shoulder and watched the fire burn ever lower.

"Sarah…"

"Yes?" She lifted her head to meet his eyes.

His lips against hers were the only answer she received. In

one fluid, effortless movement, he swept her up into his arms and carried her to the bedroom. Sarah's mind spun, but there was no defined thought. Her heart pounded with ferocity as he set her down on the bed and she lay back against the pillows. He kicked off his boots and she reached out to close the gap between them as he climbed into bed beside her.

She locked down the door inside that led to Daniel and, for the first time, she was just Sarah. Jack's fingers intertwined with hers as their lips met and she dissolved into him.

FOURTEEN

SARAH WOKE TO a room swelling with sunshine and the rhythm of fingers running through her hair. With a leisurely stretch, she rolled to face Jack.

"Good morning," he answered, smoothing hair away from her face. "Sleep well?"

"Mmmmmm…" was all she could muster, but her smile was answer enough for him.

"Food or shower?"

"Do we have to get up?"

"Sorry, love, but I promised Fred I'd fix their shower this morning."

Sarah snuggled closer to Jack, winding the covers more tightly around the both of them and making sounds of protest. He wound his fingers in her hair and pulled her in for a long kiss.

"Okay, we've got to get up or I'll never leave this bed."

"I'm all right with that," Sarah attempted distraction with more kisses.

"Ahhh, you're killing me."

"Fine," Sarah flung away the covers. "You shower, I'll cook."

Jack watched from the bed as Sarah slid into slippers and wrapped a worn cardigan around her athletic frame before jumping out of bed himself and headed to the bathroom.

"Sure you don't want to join me?"

"No, I'm not sure at all, but now that I've thought about pancakes, I'm starving."

He laughed as he closed the door and she had to shake herself to get the butterflies in her stomach under control. Whipping her hair around into a messy bun, she headed to the kitchen… then froze.

Daniel stood at the sink; arms braced, and staring out at the lake through the window.

"That's it then."

"What is 'it', Daniel?"

"You've chosen."

"Chosen? What are you talking about?"

"Do you really think he can take my place?" Daniel finally turned to face her, his blue eyes brighter from the tears in his eyes. "Do you want to force me out?"

"How can you say that? Nothing… *nothing* can take your

place!"

"He thinks he knows you so well. He doesn't know you at all... not like I know you."

"And he never will, Daniel."

"You don't know him either."

"I don't understand where you're going with this."

"You're choosing a stranger over me."

"He's not a stranger, Daniel. You loved him once; don't you want him to be happy too?"

"It's not about happiness. There's only so much room inside your head that I can get into and you're filling it up with him. You're squeezing me out." Sarah could hear the sob forming in his throat as he turned back towards the window.

"I'm not." Sarah laid her head on his hunched shoulder. "I'm not trying to... tell me what to do."

"I can't tell you."

"Sarah? Who are you talking to?" Jack emerged from the hall, barefoot in jeans, roughly drying his hair with a towel. Her head spun to Jack and then back to Daniel, but there was nothing left of him but emptiness.

"Nobody. Just talking out loud." She made her best effort to smile as he crossed the room with only the wadded up towel obscuring his chest. He pulled her close and enveloped her in his arms, tucking his head into her neck, swaying their bodies gently side to side.

"Good morning, Nobody. I hope you are having as

amazing a morning as I am," he said to the space in front of the kitchen sink. Drawing Sarah even closer, his gaze bored deep into her eyes, "and I hope *you* are having a good morning, too."

He moved to meet her lips, but without thought or hesitation, she side stepped out of his grip.

"What's wrong?"

"Nothing… I mean, I'm sorry. I just can't."

"Sorry, I guess I'm getting all the signals wrong."

"You're not… it's just…" she hesitated until he spoke again.

"Talk to me." Jack reached towards her, but decided against it, letting his hand fall back to his side.

"I can't do it to Daniel."

"Daniel? I don't get it, Sarah. How is it every time I think we're getting closer, you suddenly manage to make me feel like there are three of us in this room?"

"You can't possibly understand."

"What? What don't I understand? That you loved your brother? That you miss him? That it hurts like crazy? I think I understand losing people, Sarah. Burying all the people I love… watching them fade away before my eyes not being able to do a damn thing to save them. No. No, you're right. I don't know a damn thing about what that's like."

"That's not what I meant!"

"Then what, Sarah? Freaking explain it to me."

"He's my soul, damn it! He *is* me. I *am* him! Without him,

I'm half a person. I can't explain it any other way! Making sure he was okay, making sure his bills got paid and there was food in his fridge. Every decision I've made my whole life was based on what was best for us. How can I just turn that off? Just abandon him and..."

"Daniel is DEAD, Sarah. You can't betray a jar of ashes! Him dying is the best thing he's ever done for you."

His words were an electric current, stabbing through Sarah's stomach, striking fire to the tight bow at her core. Each fiber that ignited curled away from the whole until it was only held taut by a few singed threads. She stared at the lake through the kitchen window to maintain balance until the fire ebbed enough to allow words to come.

"How could you?"

"It's the truth, Sarah! Do I really have to yell for you to hear me?"

"Get out…"

"I'm not leaving. I'm not standing here, trying to shake some sense into you, because I'm so indifferent that I'd just walk away when things get hard."

"Fine… I'll leave."

Her slippered feet carried her to the end of the dock before she put any thought into the freezing temperature and the icy winds whipping off the lake. In the distance she could hear Jack calling for her to come back. She imagined him standing in only his jeans on the unshoveled porch, but quickly forced the image aside. She wrapped the loosely knit cardigan more tightly around her body refusing to give into the cold and return to the cabin.

Soon his boots stamped in a rapid beat down the wooden path to where she stood. Sarah had locked her feet in place, bracing for his impact, but resolutely decided in her plan to remain silent. She withdrew into Daniel's place in her mind and slammed the door behind her. It was warmer there and she could only hear Jack's reasoning and pleading as a distant detached echo. Eventually, as the pattern of boot steps moved farther away, she opened the door a crack and heard him call back to her.

"Fine, I'll go, just get inside!"

She waited until she heard the roar of an engine coming to life and the spinning of tires in the loose snow before she climbed out of her own mind and back into her body, chilled to the core.

I knew he'd leave you. Daniel's voice was more matter-of-fact than sympathetic. *Let's get you warm.*

Sarah numbly obeyed, walked back inside and fell to her knees on the rug in front of the fire, tuning into the now silent area of her mind to find Daniel, and trying to get the sweet smell of Jack out of her lungs.

FIFTEEN

―――――――

SARAH KNELT BEFORE the cold fireplace, the embers long burnt away, until her feet went numb and the braided pattern of the rug was etched into her shins and knees. Would be ghosts spun around the room, but she couldn't be bothered to glance to her left or right. Her calves and thighs protested the posture, but Sarah would not relent to move until the pain spread up her back and neck and the only answer left was to stand. On bloodless feet, she sprung up and fell back onto the couch where the tears of a thousand days threatened to overtake her. She focused instead on the excruciating pins and needles seizing her legs from the tips of her toes to her knees. Standing again as soon as she deemed her legs passable, Sarah knew what was left to do. Leave.

Wiping away any further thought she sprung into motion. Going through the checklist embedded in her mind for closing up the cabin she worked her way through each room. Sarah dumped all the contents of the refrigerator into a trash bag and tossed it into the truck bed to drop off at the dump on the way out of town. Her bedroom was saved for last, with its bed in the disarray they'd left it in. Sarah could hardly believe that she'd been so happy just hours before. She ripped off the sheets and remade the bed.

Packing wasn't hard since she'd never really unpacked the few bags she'd brought. Dressing with haste, Sarah shoved the last of the straggling items into her bag and pulled on her winter boots and Daniel's jacket. Without a glance back and in one trip, she hauled her bags and the box of Daniel's things, still sealed with evidence tape, out to the truck.

The sound of the engine echoed loudly against the silent snowy morning. She scraped at the ice on the windshield, waiting for the truck to warm up before driving away. The evidence of Jack's tires peeling out at the main road gave a twinge that she swiftly shoved away. Sarah followed his set of tire tracks all the way to Main Street and stopped. The tracks continued on into the distance like arrows pointing directly to Jack. For a moment all she wanted was to keep following them.

Do you really think he can take my place?

Daniel's words hammered at her heart and she jerked the steering wheel into a left hand turn. It was still early as the little village unfolded before her. She saw Beth just a few buildings ahead unlocking the doors to the chapel and slip inside. As much as she wanted to have Geneva behind her, Sarah had to say goodbye to Beth. She pulled the truck up to the curb and slid out, crunching through ice and snow towards the chapel doors.

Warmth soothed her aching cheeks as soon as she stepped inside. The dim morning light twisted dust motes and a sweet smell enveloped her like a familiar blanket. The last time she'd been in this chapel she'd walked in holding her mother's hand. She stood captivated by the undulating colors on the stained glass windows running the length of each side aisle.

"Sarah? Is that you?"

Sarah hadn't even seen Beth kneeling in the front pew, but now she was walking back down the aisle to greet her.

"Sorry to disturb you, I... I just wanted to let you know that I'm leaving town."

"Why so sudden? Is everything all right?"

"Yeah, I... it's just time I think. There's a lot I need to do and I've been out of the office for so long now."

"Come and sit for a second."

Sarah obeyed as Beth guided her into the back pew.

"This is about Jack, isn't it? Did something happen?"

Sarah didn't want to lie to her, but didn't care to divulge either, so she chose silence. Beth patted her knee as if all things unspoken were understood. They sat there for a while. Sarah watched the rays of the sun reach closer and closer to the altar. Just before the beams hit the base of the large wooden cross beside the pulpit, Beth cleared her throat.

"You know, it's easy to try and fill up hurting places with all the wrong things. Don't let Jack be filler. He loves you, of that I'm sure. But honey—and I'm not trying to get all preachy on you—it's just, it'd be better for the both of you to wait and be sure you're letting him into your heart because you love him back, not just because there's a big hole in there that needs filling."

Sarah took in her words while examining each line of her palms. Beth patted Sarah's leg one more time then stood and walked back up the aisle to the front pew.

"Now, you call me when you get to the city so I know you got there safely and you better come back and visit me sooner than later. Fred can't eat all that pie by himself, you know."

"Yes ma'am," Sarah replied almost inaudibly and slipped back out onto the icy street.

IT WASN'T LONG into the drive back to the city that Daniel's voice began to swirl around the truck's cabin. *You just need to get back into your routine. You need your work. It'll be easier in the city… no one nosing in on your every mood.* Sarah's head ached from the pounding of his words and for the first time she wished he wasn't so nearby.

A flash from her cell phone screen notified her she finally

had a decent signal. In an effort to drown out the chatter, she turned to checking voicemails.

Clark's quick and clear voice cut through Daniel's current assertion, "Hi Sarah, I've got all the final paperwork together. No rush, though. We'll take care of it when you get back to the city. Call me and let me know when you want to set up a time to meet."

Abandoning the other dozen messages, she scrolled to his contact and dialed.

"Sarah!" He answered before the second ring. "I was beginning to worry you'd never surface. Where are you?"

"On my way back into the city, actually. I should get in later tonight. I figure I'll get a room at the Plaza. Do you want to bring the paperwork to me?"

"Sure, why don't I meet you in the lobby for breakfast?"

"You could just come up. I'll order room service."

What are you doing, Sarah?! Daniel demanded as she asked herself the same question.

"I remember what 'come to my room' means, Sarah. And although it's tempting…"

"Forget it, just forget I said it. Why don't you just drop it by my office?"

Pathetic, Sarah. I never understood why you messed with that stiff at all.

"Sarah…"

"It's fine, Clark. I'm fine."

"Yeah, that's you, Sarah… always *fine*."

Sarah hung up the phone with unnecessary force and tossed it into the passenger seat. She quickly glanced back at the seat as Daniel now sat next to her, cradling his evidence box like a baby.

"You don't need him, Sarah. I'm here."

"Yeah, but for how long? You keep disappearing."

"I'm always here… so why the Plaza? Let's just go home."

"No, I can't go home yet. Not yet."

Daniel was quiet for the rest of the trip causing Sarah to glance back at the passenger seat from time to time to make sure he was still there. He'd never sat so still in real life. They could go days without saying a word, but couldn't go an hour without sending some kind of communication from inside. Daniel was completely silent, though, and still as a statue.

As the lights of the city drew closer, Daniel slowly faded beside her. Sarah pulled up to the valet at the Plaza and headed into the lobby while the bell staff loaded her things onto a cart. With the swipe of a credit card, she was ushered to a suite and her bags deposited without ceremony at the front door at her request. She paced the rooms. It was too bright or too clean… she couldn't figure out just what it was, but the feeling of being alone again, that was familiar.

Remembering her promise, she dialed Fred and Beth's number.

"Hello?" Jack's voice took away her words.

"Uh... um..."

"Sarah? Sarah, are you okay?"

"Yeah, just... just tell Beth I made it safely."

"Where are you, Sarah?"

"Just tell her, okay?" and without waiting she disconnected the call and turned off the phone so he couldn't call her back.

The hollow ache in the pit of her stomach returned. Nausea swept over her as waves of grief overwhelmed her once more, as severe as when she'd first seen Daniel's lifeless body. There was nowhere she could hide, it seemed. She pulled Daniel's coat more tightly around her and sat cross-legged on the bathroom floor just in case the nausea got worse. Eventually she curled up, rested her cheek on the cool marble floor, and drifted into a restless sleep.

"ROOM SERVICE," CALLED an overly perky voice between knocks.

"Come in," Sarah called, gathering herself together and smoothing her hair back out of her face. A quick glance at the mirror solidified that she looked even worse than she felt. She greeted the bellhop with a half-hearted smile and a crumpled twenty.

"Thank you." He backed towards the door with a look of concern, "is there anything else I can get you? Anything I can do?"

"No, thanks. Coffee is all that can save me now." She tried her best at a sincere grin, but suspected she failed since the worried look didn't leave his face as he closed the door.

Sarah poured a cup of coffee and picked at a piece of toast before abandoning it to focus solely on the coffee. She scoured every corner of her mind in search of a next step, but the only thing that came was Daniel's advice to get back to normal. Powering on her phone, she called Marie Claire.

"Miss Sarah!"

"Already at the office? Someone should tell your boss not to be such a slave driver." The rhythm of her business persona returned, just like slipping on a well-worn sweater.

"Oh, it's nothing. You know I love my job."

"Well, that's good because I'm back in town, so I need you to get my calendar sorted. I know we're facing a backlog so I want to get at it all right away."

"You're back? Oh... okay..." she stammered and Sarah could hear the sudden rustling of papers. "I'll start scheduling things right away. You want me to keep it slow this week? Ease you back into things?"

"No, it's all right. Let's just get back to business as usual. I'll be there within the hour."

"Yes, ma'am! I'll have your March calendar filled up in no time!"

Sarah dumped the contents of her bags to find something office suitable amongst the jeans and oversized sweaters.

Settling on a pair of gray cords and a black turtleneck, she rushed through a steaming shower. She pulled her wet hair into a bun and did her best to mask the redness in her cheek left by her marble pillow with makeup and hid the circles under her eyes under a thick layer of concealer. On final examination in the mirror, she decided it was as good as it was going to get, wrapped on her thick scarf and jacket, and lugged her laptop bag out the door.

Once at the office, she avoided sidelong glances and threw herself into emails and dug her desk out from under stacks of manuscripts and paperwork. Marie Claire kept a steady stream of coffee coming and meetings seemed to breed across her calendar. Sarah was actually glad to not have a single idle moment. She worked until even the sound of vacuums ebbed and the cleaning crew was gone.

When Sarah caught herself in an extended blink, she packed up and caught a cab back to the hotel. The silent moments alone in the suite haunted her. Daniel was far away if she could feel him at all. The past few months at the cabin felt like a dream. Jack's face fading like fog as the sun rises. The pain in her chest returned, the burning open wound she thought had nearly disappeared. She curled up under the down comforter, still wrapped in Daniel's jacket from the trip from the office, and slept.

SIXTEEN

SARAH MADE NO special effort to see Clark over the following days, leaving Marie Claire to squeeze him in
between other long overdue appointments. She'd put him and
his paperwork so far out of her mind that she jumped out of
her seat when she looked up to see him standing in front of
her desk with two lattes.

"Are you trying to freaking kill me?!"

"Sorry! Marie Claire just said to go ahead and come in."

"Geez…" Sarah gathered her chair that she'd sent rolling
away when she shot out of it. "Well, sit down." Clark gazed at
her as if waiting for another outburst then took a seat, sliding
the coffee cup tentatively towards Sarah. He looked the same
as always, but older somehow. The wedding ring on his left
hand more evident and more white appeared in his hair than
she'd ever noticed.

"On second thought, the extra caffeine might not be the best idea. I didn't mean to startle you."

"It's… it's fine." Sarah took a breath to gain composure and readjusted her blazer. "Sorry. Thanks for the coffee."

"You're welcome."

"So. Paperwork. Where do we start?" She put her best business face on, but could feel Clark's knowing eyes boring straight through it to the shades of embarrassment from their last conversation.

"I think we should talk about our phone call the other night."

"No, Clark, we shouldn't. I lost my mind for a minute, okay?" She snatched up the coffee and took a sip. The fact that it was exactly the way she liked it only added to her irritation.

"Alright then, I guess it's on to paperwork." Clark pulled a fat stack of documents bound with binder clips and covered in signature labels from his briefcase.

He pushed one document after another in front of her, explaining what each one was about and what it did. Each signature cut through the few remaining strands that tied Daniel to the world. All his things had been packed up and moved from his building in White Plains to the apartment. Trusts and deeds and titles had all been rewritten or transferred. Clark had even lined up a cash buyer for the building. Sarah signed an agreement to the offer and it was done. There was nothing left to do. All that was left of Daniel was a room packed with boxes of his things back at the apartment she couldn't bring herself to return to.

"Um, one more thing. I couldn't really figure out the best way to deliver this, but I didn't want to send it by courier or anything." He slid a brown shopping bag across the desk towards Sarah.

"What's this?" Sarah reached into the bag and her fingers met the cool metal of a tall smooth urn. She retracted her hand.

"I couldn't just leave it at the mortuary."

"No, thank you for bringing it." She pulled the bag from the tabletop and set it on the floor beside her, refusing to look inside or remove the contents.

She sat gripping the still full coffee cup, now cold to the touch, trying to stay grounded to the moment and not drift off into memories or escape into the chasm inside where she should feel Daniel, but didn't.

"You okay?" Clark finally broke the silence.

"I really wish people would stop asking that. I'm fine." She took a second sip of the cold coffee as a show of functionality.

"Usually people ask it because they can tell that someone isn't okay."

"Then why ask? Really! Should I be okay? I have my brother's ashes in a tin can. Can you make that okay?" The words poured out with more anger than she'd anticipated. "Clark…" she met his eyes and continued in a defeated tone,

"I'm sorry."

"Don't apologize to me. I'm glad to finally see you upset." He cracked a hesitant grin. "So, what are you going to do now?"

"Work," she thought for a moment. "Guess I'll eventually go home. Sort of tempted to just leave the place locked up and stay at the Plaza forever."

"Sad thing is I know you're not joking." Clark's grin stayed put, but his eyes grew sad as he gathered the papers and stood to leave.

EVERY EVENING FOR a week, Sarah resolved to return to her apartment when she left the office, if only to pack up some work clothes. Each night she would get closer. The first night, she only made it to the subway entrance. The next, she rode all the way to her stop then stayed on and caught a cab three stops down the line. Finally, she made it all the way to her block, toting Daniel's ashes the whole while, when she stopped in her tracks and turned around.

Sarah, let's go home.

I can't Daniel. Not yet.

Try.

She stopped again so quickly that the man walking behind her nearly knocked her over when she slowed his momentum. She pivoted on her heels again and walked back towards her

building. She could see the lights of the lobby and the door-
man opening a cab door for a fellow tenant. Panic seized her
and again, she froze, her arm shooting out to hail a cab.

Not tonight, she told the echo of Daniel. *Please, don't make
me.*

CELESTE WAS PERCHED on the corner of Sarah's desk, a mug of
coffee in hand, when she got to the office the next morning.

"So, have you been avoiding me or are you really that
busy?" Celeste teased.

"No, of course I haven't been avoiding you. I'm just trying to get caught up." Sarah hung Daniel's coat and avoided
Celeste's eyes.

"Marie Claire tells me you are staying at The Plaza."

"Yes." Sarah wondered where this was going.

"She also told me she's seen you pacing up and down
your block the last few nights only to catch a cab." Celeste
removed her glasses and settled into a chair.

"Did you have her tail me, Celeste?" Sarah tried to keep
the irritation out of her voice, but she couldn't help sounding
defensive.

"I'm not that nosy and she's not that clever. Apparently
she's dating a bellhop at the Trump Hotel next door."

"Hmm. Okay."

"I'm just… *we* are worried about you. You know you can

stay with me if you don't want to go home. It's understandable.
I just hate the idea of you all alone in a hotel room."

"I'm fine, Celeste, but thanks for the offer." Sarah did her
best to show appreciation with her smile, but she wasn't sure
it worked.

"All right. I'll let you get to it. Let's get lunch this week,
but if you need any help, going through his things or anything,
you just let me know, okay?"

"Sure, thanks." With people watching she didn't have
much of a choice but to go home if she was going to convince
people, and herself, that things were back to normal. Sarah
sent Marie Claire over to The Plaza in the early afternoon
to close out her bill and have her things packed and sent to
the apartment. She did her best to distract herself by wad-
ing through pages of mediocre manuscripts, but ended up
watching the New York skyline grow dimmer into the early
evening. Without further excuses, she slid the laptop into her
bag, pulled on her jacket and made the trip home.

DANIEL AND SARAH had left the apartment sterile for a reason.
It kept the memories at bay, but with a brushed nickel urn
resting on the desk ringed by a woven strand of daisies that
could only have been left by Marie Claire, even the stark
white walls couldn't hold the pain back. The evidence box
lay unopened on the floor next to the desk.

Suddenly the need to know what she'd kept at arm's length for so long was unbearable. Her knees gave out under her and she fell into a cross-legged pile beside the box, ripping away the sealing tape without ceremony and tossing aside the lid. She removed the sealed baggies one at a time. Daniel's laptop, plastered with a bright green "Keep Vermont Weird" bumper sticker. His cell phone, scratched, battered, and still without a case even through Sarah had reminded Daniel over and over to pick one up. Various random things including a framed picture of the two of them. Sarah wondered why they were considered "evidence" at all. There was a photograph of the gun that ended things, cleaned up and looking innocuous, attached to the forms she would need to retrieve the gun. The thought of ever holding the cold metal in her hand sent visions of Daniel's last moments and a roll of nausea passed through her.

Visions came in flashes, pulling the gun out from under the mattress, leaning against the wall and sliding to a seated position on the floor, tears streaming down his cheeks, kissing the letter in his left hand.

"I love you, Sarah. I'm sorry." Daniel angled the gun in his last act and all went black.

Sarah opened her eyes, returning to the floor of her apartment, and it was in her hand, the unfolded letter preserved in plastic, the writing so familiar it could be her own. Her heart stopped beating and the place of connection inside was silent as a tomb.

Her eyes raced down the page but it wasn't a letter at all. It started off "Dear Sarah" and ended "Only Yours, Daniel", but the words in between… they were the lyrics to his favorite Tom Petty Song.

She wore faded jeans and soft black leather
She had eyes so blue they looked like weather
When she needed me I wasn't around
That's the way it goes, it'll all work out

There were times apart, there were times together
I was pledged to her for worse or better
When it mattered most I let her down
That's the way it goes, it'll all work out

It'll all work out eventually
Better off with him than here with me

It'll all work out eventually
Maybe better off with him than here with me

Now the wind is high and the rain is heavy
And the water's rising in the levee
Still I think of her when the sun goes down
It never goes away, but it all works out.

Sarah hadn't spent much time thinking about what would
Sarah hadn't spent much time thinking about what would be
in that letter, but this certainly wasn't what she'd expected.
She wanted to know why; to read every bit of what he'd been
thinking and feeling to make him do this, but Daniel gave
her none of this. Shots rang through her chest and anger rose
along with the bile in her stomach. She made a sprint for the
nearest bathroom. Memories forced their way back up to the
surface. Warm summers, cold winters, her mother brushing her
hair, her father pushing Daniel on a swing, both their parents
smiling widely as they snapped photos of the twins dressed up
for prom. Two closed caskets at the front of a church. Daniel's
slumped body. Sarah holding Daniel in an emergency room
as he rocked and sobbed and cried, "It's all my fault" over and
over again… then she dissolved into the memories.

SEVENTEEN

DANIEL, SARAH AND their parents had escaped yet another renovation of their New York apartment with a long weekend at the cabin to celebrate the twins' 18th birthday. They stopped in Stowe for a special dinner at their favorite restaurant before driving the rest of the way to Geneva. Daniel had planned to tell their parents on the last night of the trip since he and Sarah would be leaving the next day for a trip across Europe, but instead he seized the public opportunity, hoping the crowd would mitigate any real outburst. Knowing what was coming, Sarah's stomach grew more tense as the evening wore on. She always was the one to bear the worry for both of them.

Over dessert, in a casual tone that only he could muster for such serious news, Daniel told his parents that he was in love with a boy. Without a word, their father stood up and walked to the bar, returning with a bottle of gin, a glass of ice and an uncanny grimace. Daniel and Sarah sat in silent observation of their father's speedy alcohol consumption and their mother's despondent gaze, first at Daniel then at her husband then back to Daniel. Sarah squeezed Daniel's hand and held her breath until their father began.

There had never been such an embarrassing scene involving a red faced father and a crying mother. Daniel sat, stoic, and watched as his father's lips finally parted, ranting at full volume in the restaurant. Sarah, immediately mortified by their father's display, stood and began apologizing to the nearby patrons. She also pulled the wallet from their mother's purse and pushed several fifties into the alarmed manager's hand.

Daniel stood calmly and walked out into the night closely followed by their slightly staggering father, still cursing and spewing threats at the top of his lungs. Sarah gathered their sobbing mother and retreated through the front door, apologizing repeatedly to anyone who would make eye contact with her. As she reached the cool night air carrying the full weight of their mother, their father was already revving the car's engine. He hadn't had a drink in five years, but it affected him the way it always had: misdirected rage. With the added fury pumping the alcohol-ridden blood through his brain, Sarah knew he couldn't be trusted to drive.

Sarah caught Daniel's eyes, her heart found the steady beat of his and she felt calm again. He moved to take the weight of their mother from Sarah, but the sobbing woman jerked her arm away as if his skin had burned hers. Again, their eyes met, and his pain flowed between them, something physical, and she pulled as much toward herself as she could so that he might feel some relief. Sarah managed to get their mother in the front passenger seat then was slapped away when she tried to reach for the seat belt.

Sarah and Daniel got into the back seat, shutting their doors and fastening their seat belts in unison. The engine screamed down the icy mountain roads back towards Geneva. Sarah crept her hand across the seat toward Daniel's and he instinctively moved his hand to hold hers. Inside her chest she felt Daniel's heart beating in pace with hers, and she felt waves of pain in that distinct way that she knew could only be his. She clamped down hard on the inside of her cheek to keep the tears at bay.

The car swerved unnaturally and Sarah found herself praying for their safety. Daniel's lips moved slightly in correspondence with her unspoken words. There was the sound of screeching tires, twisting metal, darkness and searing pain.

Their mother, thrown thirty feet through the windshield, died on impact. Their father, who'd been pinned behind the wheel when the car collided with the telephone pole, lay in a coma. Daniel refused to admit to anyone how badly he'd hurt his back. Everyone told them how lucky they were to make it out. Daniel and Sarah felt anything but lucky. They sat in motionless vigil in bloody clothes until their father's heart gave up. It took five days. They didn't speak, not even to each other.

In the months after their parents' death there was, of course, sadness, but the regret and guilt were overpowering. Sarah felt like she should have done something and Daniel believed that the only reason his father had been drunk was because of him. Sarah hated that, although she tried her best to assuage any blame, the conversation of the night had in fact been the reason their father was drinking that night. She told Daniel that if it hadn't been that night, it would have been another. It didn't matter, though, since they shared one mind and he believed with everything that their parents were gone because of who he was. Neither he nor Sarah could change that.

THE MARBLE FLOOR felt like ice underneath her legs as Sarah now sat Indian-style in the hall, the lyrics from Daniel's suicide letter still flowing through her mind. The double doors that led into her parents' suite, the rooms where all their earthly belongings had been entombed and locked away, stood before her. She longed for them now more than she'd ever allowed herself to since the day they died. The key enclosed in the wall behind her back pounded like a heartbeat in her mind.

Sarah was on her feet in an instant. She pulled a hammer out of the hall closet and swung with all her might at the spot on the wall that covered the key. With each new hole in the wall, a crack sprung open inside somewhere and grief and anger poured forth like water from a failing dam. Her cheeks were soaked in tears when she finally stopped, dropping the hammer to the floor, and she reached into the gaping hole to remove the single key hanging from a nail and stud just inside.

The key slid into the lock with ease, in no way acknowledging that it hadn't done its job in over a decade. Sarah turned the key and felt the lock click free. She rested her hands on the handles to the double doors for a long while and then, in one sudden motion, she opened them, swinging them wide so she couldn't avoid seeing what was inside.

Boxes reached toward the ceiling. Furniture gave away only outlines wrapped in dusty canvas covers. Racks upon racks of zipped up and bulging garment bags lined the walls. It really did feel like a tomb. Sarah took a tentative step towards some lower piles of boxes. The label *Photos* jumped out at her.

Tentatively, she opened the lid, inch by inch until hundreds of perfectly organized 4x6 prints came into view. Tabs titled by year and event in her mother's tidy script led the way. Sarah flipped through the memories by the handful, tears now in endless streams down her cheeks. The knot that had lived in her throat began to give up its hold as she let long held sobs escape from her chest. Tears blurred her vision, but she held tight to the slices of memory that revealed a happy childhood and loving parents.

Then, even though she felt like she'd never stop crying, the sobs turned to deep breaths and the tears slowed. She continued flipping through pictures from behind a tab labeled *First Birthday*. Two babies in matching high chairs, nearly identical except for the pink frosting on Sarah's nose and the blue frosting covering Daniel's splayed fingers, smiled back at her with sparkling eyes. Their grins spread to Sarah and before she knew it, she was smiling through the steady tears.

Sarah finished that box and moved steadily through a half dozen others. Her heart was reaching out with increasing intensity for a connection to the parents she'd tried so hard to put behind her. Sarah began unzipping garment bags, breathing deeply of the long lost scent of her mother and father. The spicy tones of her father's suits, the sweet floral breeze from her mother's dresses. She'd nearly always worn dresses. Sarah had forgotten that.

"Marie Claire would die to get her hands on these dresses," she said out loud to no one in particular. An idea swept over her and she dialed the phone.

"Miss Sarah? Is everything all right?"

"Yes. Sorry to call so late."

"It's no problem."

"I know tomorrow is Saturday, but I was wondering if you would mind coming over to help me go through some things at the apartment. I have a few dozen vintage dresses with your name on them."

"Of course!" Marie Claire was won over at "vintage."

"Thanks, Marie Claire. I appreciate your help. See you in the morning." Sarah hung up and made the same call to Celeste.

"I'm glad you asked, Sarah, but if you are really giving away your mother's clothes, I've got dibs on the furs."

Sarah let out a genuine laugh. "They are all yours."

With a relaxed calm in her chest she hadn't felt in ages, Sarah made tea and puttered around the apartment into the late hours, unpacking and putting things back in order. Memories of Daniel singing his Tom Petty song played in her mind like a jukebox, but it didn't hurt the way she thought it would. She thought about the words and why he would have left them for her. All she heard, over and over, though was Daniel singing, it'll all work out.

Beyond exhausted and with puffy eyes, Sarah pulled on one of Daniel's old shirts, kissed the framed family photo on her bedside then crawled into her own bed for the first time in months.

EIGHTEEN

ARIE CLAIRE AND her rampant energy arrived with coffee, breakfast sandwiches and Celeste in tow. They made no mention of Sarah's puffy eyes or disheveled hair, just hugged her tightly and set off to work. Sarah made quick work of dividing the clothing between the ladies and a charity pile. She did keep, however, a few dresses she had distinct childhood memories of longing to wear someday. One of those was her mother's wedding gown. It was uncanny how perfectly it fit. She could see the eight year old grinning madly from the mirror, the dress tied with ribbons to make it short enough, and glittery pumps 10 sizes too big.

"You look so much like your mom," Celeste smiled with eyes threatening to overflow as she watched Sarah turn circles in the beaded lace gown.

All Sarah could do was smile as she kept the same tears at

bay. A flash of Jack appeared beside her in the mirror but she pushed aside the impulse to call him.

Marie Claire's organization skills took over and soon a healthy keep pile full of favorite memories grew in the middle of the living room. Box after box, Sarah was amazed at how few personal items there were. The majority of the space was taken up with all the things her mother had ordered for the remodel that never got finished. Celeste and Marie Claire both vetoed Sarah's first instinct to give it all away. Celeste, who shared her love of interior design with Sarah's mother, ran about the apartment, surveying the stark empty rooms, and began dragging unearthed pieces of furniture to this area and that.

The apartment began to bloom with color. Throw pillows on the couch, a giant rug of blues and greens, and an entry table complete with lamps and artistically stacked "keep" books. Sarah left to pick up lunch for the crew and returned to find Marie Claire instructing two guys from maintenance what was to be picked up by the charity truck and what went to the dumpster.

"I knew I hired you for a reason," Sarah gave Marie Claire a squeeze of gratitude and she returned the gesture with a glowing grin.

Sarah leaned against the doorjamb finishing her iced tea and examining the newly decorated bedroom suite that had once been her parents' but was now filled with her favorite things. It was amazing what they accomplished in less than five hours. She'd always thought it would be a sad day when she would finally have to go through all their things, but she now felt a sense of relief and nostalgia… and love.

"Shall we start on Daniel's room?" Celeste's hand on her shoulder held her grounded when the thought of Daniel's things sent a wave of dread through her.

"Let's do it." Going through her parents' things had brought back sweet memories. She hoped going through her brother's things would do the same.

Daniel had owned even less than she imagined. Only a dozen boxes, mostly clothes, were stacked near the door. Most of the clothes were easily absorbed into Sarah's closet and CDs and movies merged with her own collection. A sizeable section of the room was stacked high with furniture she easily parted with. Taking up the most space was a dozen human sized marble statues, wrapped and crated and labeled and sealed.

"I don't know what you were thinking of doing with his statues," Marie Claire began timidly, "but that Karen lady from The Exhibition has called several times about the show Daniel was going to have. It had been scheduled for the beginning of April. It'll be a lot of last minute planning but I was just thinking that maybe it could be a cool memorial for him… I mean, people coming to pay their respects and see his work. If I was an artist, that's what I would want."

"That's a great idea!" Celeste patted Marie Claire on the

back reassuringly. "What do you think, Sarah?"

"A memorial and a fundraiser. Daniel would have loved that."

"I'll get right on it!" Marie Claire was both excited and relieved that her idea went over well.

Sarah arranged for cars for both ladies when evening set in. She let the hot water tank drain yet again as she showered and let a new set of tears swirl down the drain. It wasn't the same thrashing pain, though; just a deep sadness. It was a sadness she didn't mind so much because it was brought on by sweet memories and feelings of overwhelming love.

The apartment felt brand new after all the arranging by Celeste. Every direction she looked, there was a sliver of her past that now made her smile. Tucked into a shelf, playing bookend to a row of photo albums, was the rusty He-Man lunch box she'd brought back from the lake. Sarah traced each letter with her finger and remembered the afternoon with Jack, smashing through walls and barriers in her heart all the same time.

Today has been another wall-smashing day.

NINETEEN

O F THE DOZEN or so photos of Daniel that Sarah had given her, Marie Claire picked the one that had lived on Sarah's computer desktop for the last several years. The sun tanned version of Daniel, smiling broadly, stared back at Sarah the same way the living version of him had the day when she took the picture. There he was, printed out life size, framed and surrounded by flowers and candles, greeting everyone as they entered the gallery.

People had already arrived and were milling around the statues, some with tears in their eyes, some gathered together relating memories and telling stories that led to laughter. The walls, lined with black velvet draping and dramatic lighting highlighted the marble forms in a way she had never seen them. Sarah skirted the walls and surveyed the scene, still talking to the Daniel that hadn't spoken to her since she read his last words.

You were so talented, Daniel. You were so loved.

Each person eventually approached her, with handshakes or sobbing hugs, but all with cherished memories, bright and beautiful, of the Daniel that they wanted to remember. And although she grew weary of all the sorrys, she stood fast until she'd met and heard from every person, wanting to store up all the love, as if she could somehow hear and feel it all for Daniel.

"It all looks amazing, doesn't it?" Celeste rested an arm around Sarah's shoulder.

"It really does. Hey, I have something for you."

"For me?"

"Well, a favor really." Sarah pulled a thick manila envelope from her bag and handed it to Celeste. "Would you mind taking a look at what I've been working on?"

"You've been writing?" Celeste's smile reminded Sarah of her mother. "It would be my pleasure."

"Thanks, Celeste."

Sarah returned to greeting visitors, making her way around the room in great circles. And then she found herself facing two of the most loved faces in her life.

"Hi there, Chipmunk. How you holding up?"

"Fred! Beth!" In an instant, she had them both in an embrace and they didn't rush the release. Finally letting them breathe, she stepped back, "When did you get into town? Where are you staying? I didn't know you were coming or I would have arranged something."

"Don't you worry yourself, my dear. We just drove in this afternoon with Jack and he has us all settled into a hotel for the weekend." Beth's motherly instincts kicked in and she tucked away one of Sarah's flyaway hairs.

"Jack is here?" Sarah's gaze swung wildly around the room.

"He's, well, he wasn't really sure if you'd want him here, but we told him he had to come."

"Of course I want him here."

"That's what I told him. He's just over there." Fred pointed towards the bar with his thumb.

"You'd better go say hi so he doesn't hide there all night, dear," Beth scooted her along.

Jack didn't see her approach which gave her a moment to take in his features. He was the same Jack as always but clean-shaven. She'd never seen him dressed up before, never mind in an expensive tailored dark gray suit. She slid onto the stool beside him but he still didn't break his examination of the ice in his gin and tonic.

"I busted through another wall and thought of you," she said after a few more silent moments.

His eyes snapped to hers with a start and all he managed to get out was, "I… I…"

"Jack, I'm so sorry. About everything. And it means so much that you came tonight."

"No, Sarah, I'm sorry. I should never have said what I

did… and I shouldn't have left. And…" he regained his voice then she swiftly cut him off.

"We agree."

"Agree to what?"

"No apologies… just pie, remember?" She slid her hand over his.

A special smile played across his face as he gave her hand a squeeze. "I remember."

The evening continued with conversations with Daniel's friends and acquaintances. Eventually, the room began to clear and Jack left to drive Fred and Beth back to their hotel. Sarah milled around the statues for one last time as Karen, the curator, excitedly announced that each piece had been sold. Sarah was relieved, but sad.

She stood before the last statue Daniel made, a gift for her, she had assumed. The twins stared straight ahead with their marble eyes, and for the first time, Sarah noticed the carved ribbon tying their wrists together. The lyric *I was bound to her for worse or better* played to music in her mind. The word "was" echoed painfully in her chest.

She stepped forward and rested her hand over the stone one covering his heart.

Goodbye, my Daniel. Sarah kissed her brother's marble forehead then turned and walked out into the drizzling New York night.

Sarah ran to the door when the doorbell sounded the next morning. She greeted the three smiling faces with a genuine one of her own. Squeezing Beth, then Fred and finally Jack in turn, she led them all into the apartment and to the newly unearthed dining table set with linens and dishes that had been hiding in their packaging for over a decade.

"Well, well, Chipmunk! This is some set up you've got here!"

"Thanks! But really, you should have seen it a few weeks ago. Most of this was boxed up in my parents' room. Please, check it out, though. I'm just going to finish up breakfast."

Sarah finished bringing out the piles of pancakes and platter of eggs and sausage she'd just cooked from the kitchen counter and filled the glasses with orange juice.

"Who wants coffee?" Three cries of "yes!" sounded in unison.

"Dang, Sarah! You are dangerous with a hammer!" Jack called from the hall and followed up with laughter.

"I told you I busted through a wall! Now, come on, don't let the food get cold."

The little family settled in around the table and without a thought, joined hands while Fred blessed the food, this new home, and their time together.

There was still crispness to the air even though spring was in full season. Jack and Sarah, full on pancakes and coffee, strolled without aim or direction through the park after sending Fred and Beth off on a horse-drawn carriage ride. It didn't take long for their hands to find each other and the warmth Sarah had always felt there.

"Let's sit down." Sarah pulled Jack towards a bench.

"What's up?"

"This is for your camp," Sarah pulled an envelope from her jacket pocket and placed it on Jack's lap.

"I can't take your money, Sarah."

"You didn't even open it! You don't know that it's money."

"What else would fit in an envelope?" His raised eyebrow made her smile.

"Open it or not, but you have to accept it. It's not really from me anyways."

"Then who is it from?"

"Daniel." When Jack remained speechless, she continued, "It's the money we raised with the sale of his statues. He would have loved what you are doing, Jack. I know it's what he would have wanted."

"Then I'll take it… for Daniel."

"So, what's next?"

"Well, the first round of campers will be coming the last week of May. I'm down to final touches. I've even got a team of counselors lined up. What about you?"

"I think I need to stick around a while. Get used to being

in the city again. Get back into a work routine."

"So you aren't moving to the lake."

"Not now. Not *no*, just not now. I'll be back though. I want to be there for your grand opening and to scatter Daniel's ashes."

"And what about us? Where are we?"

"I care about you, Jack. A lot. I just think we should take things slow for a while. See where it goes from here."

"I care about you, too." His special smile spread wildly across his face. "And I agree about taking things slow. So slow in fact that I don't think I'll make the moves on you again until I've put a ring on that finger just so I'm sure you won't run away."

"Oh, that's nice!" She jabbed him in the ribs only to make him laugh harder. "So," she locked eyes with him once again, "you think you'll put a ring on this finger, huh?"

"Well, when I met your friend Marie Claire at the memorial last night, she did go on and on about how amazing you looked in your mother's wedding dress."

TWENTY

SNOW TURNED INTO rain and the thick white blanket quickly became slush, then mud. Without an effort, the earth began to pour forth green sprouts and the gray and brown trees slowly woke from their slumber setting a ripple of green across the landscape. Spring was in full bloom around Lake Geneva and it felt like the perfect time for this last step.

Sarah, Fred, Beth, Jack, and several other people from town set off from their various docks in canoes, kayaks and fishing boats to meet up at the center of the lake at sunset. Beth sang an old hymn and Fred said a prayer. Jack simply said, "I'll miss you, buddy," and sent three origami boats sailing. And with that, Sarah removed the lid of the urn and let loose the contents into the deep waters. The ashes of Daniel, who had once wished to be sky and mountain, dissolved into the lake like the elements were always made to be one.

Sarah watched the horizon as each ray of the fading sun slid behind pink and purple tinted clouds, Daniel's last words to her played in her mind… *Still I think of her when the sun goes down. It never goes away, but it all works out.*

THE END